AF426473

UNEXPECTED BABY FOR MY BROTHER'S BEST FRIEND

CALLIE STEVENS

Copyright © 2022 by Callie Stevens

All rights reserved.

No part of this book may be reproduced in any form or by any electronic or mechanical means, including information storage and retrieval systems, without written permission from the author, except for the use of brief quotations in a book review.

1

DYLAN

The soft music playing in the background as I write down the lyrics to my new song is my motivation. I always enjoy light upbeat tempo, and the bass guitar sounds. It is why I love *The Beatles*, regardless of how old-school modern-day rock bands consider them to be. They are my inspiration.

I was in the ninth grade when I first discovered my passion for music. It was also the year I met Lucas for the first time. A perfect guitarist and best wingman. Together, we grew up, made music, and had fun. It's funny how the best things in life happen when you least expect them. My journey with Lucas has been just that.

We are different in many ways, with music the one thing that makes us connect. But while Lucas enjoys the full life of our popularity and the benefits, I prefer to remain in the comfort of my room and make music.

"Hey D-man, come on." Speak of the devil. Glancing beyond the balcony of my suite, I spot him outside, along with his fiancée, Mika Robertson, and our band mates.

They are all dressed for the beach and Mika is clinging to his arm, like always, as he is speaking to Chase and Jay.

"Dylan, let's go," Lucas calls again, looking up at where I am. "You've been in there all day."

Resigned, I stand up and walk to the balcony so I don't have to shout. The smile on my face stays wide, but Lucas frowns at me. "You promised to make this trip fun," he complains.

"Yeah, D. You know what they say about all work no play, right? Get your ass down here and let's go!" Chase adds.

"Tonight, I promise. I just need to perfect some notes on the demo. Trust me, we'll rock and roll tonight." Winking at Mika, I add, "I promise, Mika. I know I owe you."

"Whatever, D-man." Jay dismisses me. Turning to the guys, he says, "I can only imagine what, or should I say *who* he is working on." Laughing, they turn and walk away. Always the prankster, that Jay. Shaking my head, I go back inside to the comfort of my solitude again.

Relief fills me as I sit on my chair, face the mirror, and begin practicing the lyrics for the demo.

"Late nights ... I love the late nights with you." The sound of my voice, the melody from my guitar, and my foot tapping on the ground bring the melody to light.

Perfecting my music is my life; it is all I can think of doing most of the time. And as much as I enjoy spending time with my friends, and especially hanging out with Lucas, making sure our band is successful is still the number one goal for me.

It's the only way I can have the platform to help the people who need a voice.

Also, I enjoy the golden silence of being alone. It helps me think ... helps me plan.

There's one note that's not quite right, yet, or I'm not quite hitting it. Groaning, I start from the beginning. Again. Taking my time to perfect the tone I want for the bridge of the song. Playing the guitar makes me feel alive, and as I approach the high rock part of the song, I feel my nerves settle inside me.

For years, my peace, my escape came from music. At fourteen, it was the one thing that kept me afloat. *"Your son's borderline depressed, and I think music keeps him going."*

Not like my mother cared what the therapist she was making me see twice a week thought when she came for a joint session. And she let me know just what she thought about it when we got home that day. She had two settings with me: caring mother for the public eye, and insults or just plain right ignoring me the rest of the time. I preferred when she ignored me. It hurt less.

The therapist had been right about so many things, but none of it mattered in the end, because when I reached fifteen, my mom said there was no need for the therapy sessions anymore. So, just as it had started, my therapy stopped. No regard for what I wanted or needed. It was never about that.

Playing at the back-alley club down the street where we lived in San Jose became my new therapy. I didn't need to listen to my mother's constant nagging, the loud noises when my parents got into a fight, or the harsh words whenever she was in one of her moods, as Dad called them.

I found solace at that bar. With Lucas, Jay, and Chase, I found my happy place.

Music.

I can't imagine doing anything else. At seventeen, when I moved out of my parents' house, my father finally found the courage to ask for a divorce. I suspected my mother would put up a fight, like she always did when she wanted to have her way, but none came.

Their divorce had been silent. Papers were signed, and I never had to see her again. Neither did my father. It had been all over. And yet, fifteen years later, I'm still somewhat that little boy who hated loud sounds and raised voices. Ironic considering my line of work, but when I'm singing and playing, my mind is somewhere else. However, I rarely ever enjoy hanging out in bars.

My cell phone buzzes on the table, distracting me from my thoughts, and I pick it up. "Ken," I say as I rub the back of my neck. "How's it going?"

"Great," Ken Daystar, our manager, and number one fan, answers in a light tone. "Lucas and the others?"

"Having fun someplace at the beach," I reply.

"And you? Who do you have beside you right now? Blonde or redhead?"

I laugh at Ken's question, then shake my head and stroke my jaw. Ken thinks I'm a major player. That I am always with a different girl anytime I'm not with the guys. I don't correct his assumptions.

"Blonde," I reply, glancing at the poster of Gwen Stefani on my wall. She is my number one celebrity crush and blonde as can be, so it's not like I'm lying.

"Great, don't forget, two weeks and we need you back for the tour," Ken says. "With Lucas out on his honeymoon, we will need you to cover for him for a couple of shows. Think that will work?"

The plan is for Lucas to join us by the time we get to Wyoming. With me as the lead guitar player and second voice, I usually leave the lead singing to him. Not having him there means I'm stuck as lead singer and lead guitar since Chase is our drummer and Jay plays the bass.

Double the fun for me, right?

He doesn't give me time to answer. "Either way, congratulate Lucas for me. I should join you all on the island before the wedding."

"Will do, talk later."

He drops the call, and I drop my phone on the table, place my guitar on the bed, then rub the back of my neck. Rising to my feet, I stretch my muscles for a bit to release the cramps starting to build up on my shoulders.

Guess I should join the others. I take off my shirt and walk to my bathroom for a quick shower.

Lucas and Mika excuse themselves and leave. Jay and Chase left earlier to go to a club they heard was pumping nearby. Those two are party animals. I'm nursing my third glass of brandy, the same one I had just started when the happy couple decided to call it a night, enjoying the light music in the bar, and thinking it is time to call it quits too when a group of people walks in. *Guess the night is just starting for some people.*

My eyes immediately land on two girls coming in. Specifically a woman with dirty blonde hair waving down her back and a killer smile. She is facing my way, and I'm blown away by the sparkle in her eyes.

A rush of adrenaline suddenly flows through me. Though beautiful women are always surrounding us when we play, that doesn't make me appreciate true beauty any less. And unfortunately, no matter how I act, as soon as they find out what I do for a living, they always have one impression of me.

Playboy.

Regardless of how nice or how rough I act, though, they love the attention they can get from hanging out around me. Which is not surprising either. Women are fickle. I often wonder how people manage to find just one to stick with.

And it's not that I have a thing against commitment, love, or big weddings. Lucas is all in that scene and I am happy for him. I can tell he loves Mika very much, and I like her too because she is one of the few good women I have met, but that's just it.

Besides Mika and Carol, Lucas's mom, I never keep any other women around long enough to know what they are like. We meet, have a fun time together, and on they go.

I respect them and admire them, but that is it. There is no point in losing myself, like my father did, or risking the heartbreak that comes with it.

It's not worth it.

So, I always keep a clear head. I'm always honest about how things are, and we keep things simple and easy. I empty my glass and stand up. I can't take my eyes off this blonde.

She laughs again. Somehow, her deep timbre reaches me and it's like every other noise around me fades away. Like a parched man to water, I can't stop myself from following the sound. As I draw closer, the woman sitting to her side stands and walks away. The blonde casts a glance over her shoulder, and her eyes briefly land on mine.

That single moment is enough to get my pulse racing and my heart thundering in my chest. It is an intense response; one I have never felt.

"No wonder the sky is dark outside," I say as I take the empty stool next to hers and order for the waiter. "All the color is in your eyes." My voice is a low, deep baritone that sounds husky even to me, but it doesn't matter because I love the tingles already racing through me when she gives me a side grin.

"That's a cheesy pick-up line," she says and looks at me again.

God, I love her eyes and her smile.

She is gorgeous. The perfect set of white teeth flashes at me. I notice the small button nose on her face and the way her brows arch softly as her eyes flicker over mine.

"You think so? I should try again, then," I answer, and she laughs.

"I was wondering if you were an artist because you were drawing me in," I say cheekily. She laughs.

"Wait. I have another one. We are not socks, but we'd still make a great pair. How's that?" I lay it on really thick, with a smile on my lips.

"That's so bad," she replies, still laughing. "Does that work for you?"

"Every time," I say. "I mean it, though," I add when she laughs again. "I can't take my eyes off you. I think it's your eyes ... or maybe your smile. Either way, you're the most beautiful woman I have seen here tonight."

Her laugh mesmerizes me for a second. The effect is even stronger at close range and I can't help but feel like I have superpowers for making her laugh so much in just these couple of minutes.

"Tonight, huh? I see. Do you keep a tally every night?"

"Oh, no. This is definitely a special night," I play along. She has spunk and I find I'm even more intrigued by the beauty before me.

"Oh yeah? And what's so special about tonight?"

"You're here." And I thank the rock gods that I decided to join my friends tonight.

"Flattering," she says. "I like it. And I like you."

She turns back to the table and picks up her glass. The waiter arrives in front of us then, and I ask her, "Let me buy you a drink, and then you can tell me what your story is."

"What makes you think I have one?"

"You're at a bar, drinking alone ... It's either, you're done with one relationship or you're scouting for another."

The waiter pours us a drink and I down mine in one go. She does the same, and orders for another. I discreetly notice the rings on her fingers. Her hands are slender, her nails a hot, red shade that makes my blood start to hum with a low wave of desire as I imagine them scratching down my back while I make her scream my name.

"Are *you* scouting for another?" she asks me. When she looks at me again, her round eyes latch onto mine. There is something so intense about her gaze that a shiver races up my spine. I just can't explain it, but I sense the fire in her instantly.

The corners of my lips lift into a smile, and I shake my head. "Not at all," I say. "That's the last thing on my mind tonight.... You?"

She hesitates. I wish I knew what she's thinking because her eyes get clouded. I find myself leaning into her without even realizing it, and one more breath brings in her scent. It is intoxicating. My body comes alive and a dance of raw hunger starts inside of me.

My eyes drop to her lips. They are full, soft, and inviting. I can already imagine myself tasting them.

"No," she answers, and I pull myself back to reality and look into her eyes again. "I'm not looking for one either. Not tonight."

2

———

AMY

He has the most captivating eyes ever. His smile and small hand gestures as he talks suck up my attention. I am lost in his eyes and drowning in the sound of his voice. I instantly know this is the man I came looking for tonight.

As I sit here with him and let him pour me another drink, I remember Casey's advice to me before she ditched me for some random guy some minutes back.

Try to have fun, Amy ... It's a vacation, and you work too hard. Loosen up, get laid, maybe. I remember Casey's giggle before she left me. As if I could afford to take any time off. This might be a vacation spot, but other than the wedding party, this is business as usual for me. I'm here to work first and enjoy the island second. But then her words, *Get laid,* come back again as I look at the man before me, leaving me shuddering at the mere thought of some action with this guy. Casey thinks I've been with a few guys, but truth is, I haven't found anyone who made me want to go all the way. I have fooled around, of course. And been in a few relationships. But when push comes to shove, I have never been able to just let go and give myself to anyone. So, here I am, at twenty-two and still a virgin. How sad is that?

I look at him then, and he is staring at my lips. The first thing that crosses my mind is panic. Would I really be able to give myself away to a stranger? Even if it is this god before me?

I came here to Hawaii, regardless of the workload I have right now, for my brother's wedding. Both he and his fiancée made me promise to show up, and as the designer for the wedding dress and the groom's sister, how could I not? But the truth is, I would have preferred to avoid my mother. She is a bit too much. And now, with this wedding, I know I will never hear the end of her disappointment—that I am yet to bring any man home, or even a date for the day—all of which I am used to. Sheesh, you'd think I'm going on forty the way she talks sometimes.

My brother was always the golden boy. Mom loves him, Dad was proud of him, and it is difficult being my own person without the tag... *My brother's sister*.

I used to hate it when everyone addressed me in association with him, but with time, I learned to get over it. Making my own name and being my own person is all I want to do now, and designing this wedding dress is a huge deal for me because it can give me the exposure I need.

My fashion brand, Keaton Designs, is solely me. Keaton is my late granddad's name. He was my favorite person in the world and I was his. He always made me feel special. To him, I was always the light that shone brighter. Too bad we lost him so soon.

Shaking myself out of it, I look at the man in front of me again, and I decide maybe I can be bold and stupid for once and do something Casey would do.

"First time in Hawaii?" I ask him.

He immediately shakes his head. "Third."

"Wow, they say the third time is a charm, right? Have you found yours yet?"

The way he looks at me after that question sends a shiver down my spine. I can't tell what it is about this man that gets to me. Can it be the perfect shape of his face? Long, light brown hair tied to the back of his head, or his eyes that are a forest green shade? Or is it that voice?

It is smooth and yet terrifying. It makes my skin flush and tingle, and he hasn't even touched me yet. He lifts a hand to pick up the bottle the waiter left for us, and I move to pick up my glass at the same time. Our fingers brush and his touch on my skin lingers.

The slow hum rising in the pit of my stomach sends my pulse into a pounding rage. My nerves immediately flair. I have never felt anything like this.

"I think I found one," he says, then picks up his glass and winks at me before drinking.

My heartbeat triples and knocks the wind out of my lungs. I drink too. The fiery liquid burns a path down my throat and the impact on my head is intense.

"It's my first time in Hawaii," I tell him, then set my glass on the table. "I'm here for a wedding."

"Crazy, I'm here for one too. My best friend found his love match and they are perfect for each other."

"That sounds nice," I say.

"It does. I love that he is happy."

"But?" I ask, sensing there is more he wants to say.

He cocks a brow. "No buts."

When he doesn't add anything, I raise my left brow suspiciously.

"I mean it," he says with a smile. "No buts. I genuinely love that he is happy. I'm not some sucker who believes people can't fall in love."

"I am not either," I say, but keep my eyes on him. We stare at each other for a second and he laughs at the exact same time I burst out laughing.

"I know what you're thinking," he says, and points a finger at me. "You think I'm a playboy who doesn't think he can fall in love."

"Aren't you?' I ask. "I mean, here's one thing. The hair," I say with a hand demonstrating. "That tattoo that says, 'For the love of man,' which sounds sexist, by the way, and then there's that smile, the rings ... Everything about you screams I'd get my heart broken."

He laughs harder. "But that's only if you're looking for love. Are you?"

"No," I answer. Love is the last thing I want right now. I still have a lot to accomplish. This year, I plan to strike one major milestone and get my designs on a top fashion show like New York or Paris. Then I have to travel for shoots and deals. Love is down at the bottom of my list.

"But I'll want it someday, won't you?"

He seems to think for a second before he shrugs. "Let's just say I'm not out searching."

Our eyes meet again, and I have the feeling there is more to that story, but I say nothing.

Not my concern.

"What's with that shirt?" I ask, laughing as I point at it, letting the topic go so we can move on to lighter topics.

Time goes by unnoticed, and the bar starts to get emptier and emptier. Still, we sit there, laughing and drinking. We talk about anything and everything until he tells me about his passion for music. I can imagine him singing on a stage. His voice is lovely even when he speaks.

"Sing for me," I ask, but he shakes his head.

"You'd have to do something for me in return," he answers. I hesitate and he quickly adds, "Don't worry, it's not difficult."

"What is it?"

"Maybe I should get your word and sing first so you can't back out later," he says.

I giggle again and I press a hand to my lips. For some reason, I can't stop laughing and smiling with him.

"Alright, I'll tell you what it is first." He sighs theatrically, then shifts back on his chair. "Let me take you someplace nice tonight. I know a great spot near the beach. It's only past midnight and it's the perfect time to go there."

"You think so?" I ask.

He nods. "I promise I'll sing when we get there."

"Fine." I don't need to think twice.

Standing up, I reach for my purse, but when he puts his hand on mine, I freeze. His skin is not cool like I thought it would be. It's hot, and the warmth seeps through my skin. My fingers curl even before he tightens his grip around them and places a dollar bill on the table.

The waiter gives him a small salute as he is leading me toward the exit.

Once outside, he pulls me to a power bike and takes out some keys from his pocket. "Ever ridden one of these?"

"Yes, my brother used to have one," I reply as he hands me a helmet. I secure it on my head and wait for him to climb first.

"Hold on tight," he says to me, and my hands instinctively tighten around his midsection. Feeling the hard muscles of his rock-solid abdomen, I lick my suddenly dry lips.

My pulse starts racing again, and there's a fluttering movement inside me. The leather and wood scent combination wrecks my senses. I imagine what it would be like to touch his bare skin.

The leather jacket he is wearing is cool against my cheek as I press it onto his back. He kicks the engine of his bike alive in one start, swerves, and enters the road.

We ride for a while, and the entire time, I am melting inside. When he finally slows his ride at the beach, I get off and he takes my hand again.

He leads me toward the small stand at a distance. There is a crowd of people there, some people seated, others dancing. A band is playing, and though the music is loud, lots of laughter and the cool wind of the night make everything more charming.

"What's going on?" I ask at the top of my voice because I can barely hear myself.

He grins as he turns to me and says, "It's a live band for hula dancing."

"Hula?"

He does a small movement with his hips and hands in front of him, and oh boy, I can't hold back my laugh. He looks funny and sexy at the same time.

Cheeks wide from all the grinning, I ask. "Who taught you that?"

"It's Hawaii, everyone loves to dance," he says, then takes my hand and leads me to the dance floor.

We spend the next twenty minutes dancing and I have no idea what I'm doing. I'm just moving my hips and legs to match his rhythm and having too much fun. The best fun I have had in a while.

"Okay, I'll sing now," he says and walks to the stage. He says something to the lead singer, and they give him the mic. Then he turns and points in my direction. "This one is for you."

He starts to sing a slow song, and my heart warms as I listen to his melodious voice. The warmth spreads through me, and I love the feeling. When he ends the song, as the crowd cheers and claps for him. He comes back to my side and we sit.

"That was amazing," I tell him.

"Thank you."

We stay on the beach for a long time, just enjoying the weather, the vibe, the night. Each other. As soon as the crowd starts to disperse, I realize I drank too much. I am laughing hard as I hold onto his hand and stroll with him toward his bike.

The night's wind is heavy now, probably because we are at the beach. When he faces me as we get to his bike, the wind ruffles my hair and makes it fly all over my face.

I laugh and use both hands to arrange it. He reaches out to help me, and the minute he touches my face, something tenses in the air around us. His eyes are on mine again, and there's this magnetic pull. My blood starts to hum to the tune of desire stirring inside me, and I feel myself floating away even before his lips touch mine.

His kiss is cool, and it is the best thing I have ever tasted. His tongue sweeps over my lips and makes me shiver. Who knew a kiss could feel like this? His hands move around my waist, and he pulls me to him. I part for him and give in to the sensations wracking through me.

As his hands move up and down my back, I press into

him. The stir of his erection makes me yank my lips from his. I am panting and so is he, and he is staring deep into my eyes again.

Oh, the warmth surrounding me is unbearable. I've never been with anyone like this before. No man has stirred any feelings as powerful as this. That's why it was easy for me to focus on my career and school before that. That is why I was able to stay away from boys my age. But that's just it. This is not a boy, this is a man. All man. And I want to lose control and let myself go for one night because this man is *that* exciting.

He kisses me again and I can't deny the passion it stirs in me. His taste is addicting. The blend of rum and brandy on his lips steals every logical sense of reasoning I have left.

"The beach has a suite," he is saying as he drags his lips down to the side of my neck and feasts on the pulse there. I arch for him, giving him better access. His kisses leave me shivering.

"Hm?" I can't even form words.

"There's a suite on the beach."

I can finally make sense of what he is saying to me.

"I know," I say, but my voice is husky, and I can barely hear myself. Not sure if he heard me, I nod, moan, and then nibble on my lower lip.

He takes my hand and leads me in the direction of the magnificent building to our left. Once we get inside, he gets a key for us from the reception, and leads me upstairs. Everything is happening so fast I don't even have the time to question if I'm doing the right thing. Your first time is a big deal, but this feels so right. To be here with him now. And then the time for thinking is over because as soon as the door shuts behind us, I'm in his arms again and what was still left of my brain shuts down.

His lips dip and take mine for another kiss that leaves me breathless. Nothing else matters as I slip my hands under his shirt and touch the hard muscles of his chest.

This is it. I'm really doing this. My first time. And this is going to be the best night ever!

3

———

DYLAN

My eyes remain closed as I wake up with the taste of brandy on my lips, but it is more than just that taste that makes my skin tingle. There is the image of a woman on my mind. Long dirty blonde hair that frames her face in a side part, and the coolest shade of blue eyes I have ever seen.

Remembering the sound of her laughter makes my hand search the bed, expecting to touch her warm body, but beside me, I find only cold sheets, which makes me jerk awake.

Sitting up quickly, my eyes fully open, I look around my suite room. She is nowhere to be found, her clothes are no longer on the floor, but her scent still lingers. I can't tell if it is on my skin or on the sheets, but it is there. Lavender and a blend of jasmine.

Dropping back on the bed, I drag in a deep breath. The hints of her in the air sip into my core and stir my blood to life. Closing my eyes, I throw my arm over my head and try to replay the events of the previous night in my head.

We made it here, and I couldn't take my hands off her,

or my lips. I loved her taste, the soft sighs that left her lips as my hands moved down her body. The softness of her palms as she pressed them flat on my chest. I recall we dropped on the bed, and she lay on top of me. From then, it is a blur.

Argh. Standing up, I head to the bathroom to wash my face. I drank so much last night, we had both fallen asleep the minute we touched the bed.

Nothing happened. I raise my head and stare at my reflection in the mirror. "Shame," I whisper. The woman from last night is the sexiest being I ever met.

Everything about her is seductive. The way she moves, the sound of her voice, and even the shape of her lips.

I wonder if I will ever see her again.

Combing my fingers through my hair, I reflect on our time together last night. *I wish I knew her name.*

Crap! We didn't exchange any personal details last night. I did not ask her name and neither did she ask mine. Even if I wanted to find her, how could I?

Dragging in a deep breath, I decide to put her out of my mind as I take a shower. What are the chances of seeing her again?

That afternoon, I meet up with the boys at the beach. "Where's Mika?"

"She's with Amy," Lucas answers. He can tell I am lost, because he tilts his head to one side and clarifies, "Amy? My sister, bro."

"Oh, right," I apologize. When his words register, I frown. "Amy is in town?"

"Yeah, she came in from New York yesterday and Mika is meeting with her to test the wedding dress. My mom arrives in two days and Ken texted me to say he'll make it in time for the bachelor party."

Lucas plasters a hand over my shoulder, then smiles. "And you, my best man, need a haircut."

"No, no, not the hair," I say as he gives me a mischievous smile.

"Come on, don't be an old grump."

Lucas relaxes on his chair again and shows me a picture of Sara on his phone. "Is she the one you're bringing to the wedding?"

"Why would I?" I ask as I stare at the model I haven't seen in over two months. "I ended things with her."

"I think he's seeing a Josephine now," Jay inputs.

"Josephine?" Chase asks, then pushes his blond hair from his face pulling it back with his hand in his trademark gesture. "Wasn't it a Louisa? Or was it Anna?"

"Louisa? Anna? Or maybe the whole state of Louisiana." Jay jokes.

We laugh as I shake my head. "I'm not with anyone, relax."

"You say that every time," Lucas says.

"I mean it this time. Although I did meet someone last night and she was quite interesting."

"Who?" my friends ask, their attention pinned on me. I look into their eyes, from Lucas's curious baby blues, to Chase's warm arctic blues, and then Jay's mischievous navy blues. I guess I stand out with my often-serious forest green eyes. I love these guys like brothers, but there is no way I'm sharing last night with them. When I shrug, their disappointment is evident, and it makes me laugh. "Relax ... Lucas is the only one taken here," I say in a light tone, then sit back on my chair to enjoy the afternoon.

That evening, we drive around town, and I play my guitar in the back of Lucas's convertible. Lucas sings behind the wheel, Chase, riding shotgun, marks the beat with his drumsticks he can't seem to part with, and Jay adds to the beat with his lips and hands.

I'm having the time of my life.

"I play with the strings of your heart, and the ties of your sleeves..." The lyrics of our first single, Heart Strings, flows through the air as I play. Smiling wide, I remember what it was like to perform that song on stage for the first time.

"I never get tired of performing this song," Jay says when I finish the bridge. Nostalgic nods all around. This was our first hit and it speaks to us still. We go on to talk about the upcoming tour for a few more minutes before we arrive at our destination. I jump out of the car without opening the door, but leave my guitar inside, picking up my coat instead.

My hair is free from its usual ponytail band, and I comb my fingers through it.

"Mika keeps talking about the treats here. Let's try it out and see if we can use it for the wedding, else I'll be toast," Lucas says.

We are laughing and bantering as we enter the bakery. A woman grinning widely greets us immediately, and I look around the well-lit setting. The place is swarmed with customers. A bell rings and a woman comes out of a side door holding a tray. Lucas suddenly waves, and I turn to see him smile at Mika who is at the left end of the bakery.

"Over there," Lucas says. "Mika's sitting with Amy."

He leads the way and the rest of us follow. When we get to their table, I sit opposite Mika and smile at her. "You're shinning, Mika ... It's like you're a different person."

She smiles at my compliment, and I add. "Isn't she, Jay?"

Jay nods in agreement, then picks a serviette from the holder on the table. "She looks like she's living the dream."

Mika laughs. Lucas drapes his right hand around her neck, smothering her with a kiss. "Aww, get a room you two," the girl sitting by my side comments, and I angle my head to look at her.

"Guys, this is Amy. Remember her?" Lucas asks just as my eyes land on her. Time seems to slow down at that moment, and my heart does a backflip that leaves me breathless. Those intense blue eyes stare back at me and send a tingle through my nerves. Just like that, I'm reminded of last night. Her scent, the soft sigh of her moans, and the heat of her skin.

"Woah, Amy. You changed a lot," Chase comments.

"You're taller, too. Look at that smile. Aren't you a catch?"

Lucas smacks Jay in the arm. Chase and Jay wink at her and laugh, and continue talking to each other. In the midst of all this, all I can do is look at Amy.

How is this possible? Amy? This is little Amy? How is she Amy?

I can't believe my eyes. Looking at Lucas, I find his eyes on me and try to compose myself. "Amy?" I ask, then look at her again, pretending like the few seconds of shock didn't happen.

"She looks a bit different, doesn't she, Dylan?" Lucas asks as I slowly let my eyes drift down her face. Last night, I probably had not looked at her properly, because she is way more beautiful than I remembered. And that is wrong. Now that I know who she is, I know how old she is, and a decade separates us. What have I done? Or, I guess, what have I *almost* done?

Her lips are slightly pursed, and she is still in shock because her eyes are wide. I admire the smoothness of her skin, the soft arch of her brows, and her little button nose.

"Come on, I don't look *that* different," she replies to him and smiles. My heart melts when I see the flash of her adorable dimples. It reminds me of the breathless sound of her laughter from the previous night.

Every inch of my skin comes alive with heat, and I realize I want to hear her laugh again. Even if that's all I can have. Because there is no way we can ever repeat last night. For so many reasons, not the least of which is her age. And let's not forget her brother is my best friend.

"She's totally different," I answer Lucas. Then I can't resist teasing her. "She used to be a miniature nerd."

Chase speaks next. "Yeah, she did. Sorry, Amy." He swipes his hair back with his hand as he smiles unapologetically at her.

Jay laughs and adds, "I thought you would have conquered the world by now, evil scientist style, Amy. But you were quite the cutie then. Now you are a knock-out! So maybe the world will be at your feet soon enough." He winks at her and Lucas slaps him again.

"Dude, that's my sister."

Chase and Jay laugh along with Mika. Amy clears her throat and the blush on her face is alluring. I can't be looking at her like this so I avert my eyes as heat rushes to the back of my neck and I force on a smile and try to fit into the conversation.

My mind, however, insists on wandering off to our moment in the beach suite. She had responded to my kisses with the same feverish passion that burned through me, so why did she disappear? And why do I have to keep tormenting myself with something that can't be?

I drag in a deep breath, but instead of the crispy air, I inhale her scent. The burst of jasmine makes me shiver and my body tightens in response.

Damn it.

"The dress is amazing, babe," Mika says. "I don't want you to see it yet, though."

"Let's order some treats, then ... how about the cake you wanted me to try out?" I tune out Lucas and Mika. Jay and Chase are bantering as always and looking at the menu on their phones.

I slip my hand into my pocket and take out my phone so I can scan the menu code, too. My hand brushes over Amy's as we reach for the menu, and the feel of her skin combined with the sound of her gasp hits me right in the chest. She drops it for me, and I hesitate a little before picking it up.

As I'm scanning the menu and trying to ignore the delicacy sitting beside me, Jay and Chase stand up and walk away from the table while discussing something that I can't bother understanding. Then Lucas does the same with his hands around Mika's waist. "Where are you going?"

"We need to meet with the chef," Mika answers with a grin. "He's in that office." Mika points at a door on the other side of the bakery.

"Don't worry. You two hang out, we'll be right back," Lucas adds. And by the mischievous grin on his face, I know they probably won't be back for a long while.

Before I can say anything else, they are on their way, and I release a deep breath before turning to Amy.

She stares at me wide-eyed, and I smirk at her. "Amy Higgins, we meet again."

4

————

AMY

My cheeks burn from all the feelings swirling inside me, and I pretend to cough again, then reach for the menu. My mind is still lost in the events of last night. My insides are still immersed in the pool of desire he created in me, and it is difficult to hide my breathlessness.

"So, we're just going to pretend it didn't happen?" he asks when I don't say anything to him and focus my attention on the menu. Truth is, I'm still in shock myself. Dylan, my brother's best friend, looks different from what I remembered.

His forest green eyes are the same, but a lot has changed about him since I last saw him years ago. I was eight years old back then. A little girl who rarely saw her brother who preferred to hang out with his college friends.

Shutting my eyes for a second, I cringe inside as I remember the events of last night.

The kissing, the laughter, the way he lit up my body with each touch.

He scoffs and relaxes on the chair. My eyes drop to his lean fingers now tapping on the table.

"What would you have me do?" I turn to face him and meet his eyes. The effect is the same. My lips part and a soft breath falls out. I am suddenly so aware of my own heartbeat, and sensational warmth flooding me. "Last night didn't happen." I have to convince myself, as well as him. It couldn't have happened. I can't have felt that for him. We are totally wrong for each other. A rockstar playboy and a virgin. And he's so much older than me. Also, Lucas would kill us both. And yes, it was amazing, but we can pretend it was just a drunken dream and leave it at that.

"Didn't it?" he asks with a hint of sarcasm. A slow smile buds on his lips as he looks away, chuckles, then faces me again. "Because I still remember the taste of your lips and my disappointment when I found you gone this morning."

I gasp, and he arches a brow. "It was one night of madness," I deny again, determined not to indulge in the game I know he is trying to play. He is the forbidden fruit that will damn me for eternity.

When I woke up in his bed earlier this morning, it had taken a lot of effort to leave because my body still tingled from the pleasure he gave me.

Damn it, Amy ... How could I have not known he was Dylan? My brother's best man and best friend? Not just that, but a man a decade older than me. A scandal is the last thing I want at Lucas's wedding, and with the amount of attention Lucas and his group attract wherever they go, it is bound to happen if this gets out.

As I sit there, different scenarios play over and over in my head.

Lucas will be livid, for sure if he finds out, I think. He has always been so protective of me. *And if their fans find out?* It would be all over social media.

I groan and squeeze my eyes shut again, then shove my fingers through my hair.

When I re-open them, Dylan is still looking at me. "One night of madness, huh?" he says. "I can admit to that."

My heart does a triple slow dive in my chest, and it hammers so hard I fear it will burst out of my ribcage.

"Lucas can never find out," I say in a rush. "You know how he gets, and I'm sure you don't want a scandal, either."

"What makes you think that?" he replies in an amused tone. "This is Hawaii, and I live for scandals, in case you've forgotten."

"Oh, I haven't, trust me," I retort. Dylan has had his fair share of scandals already, more than all the other band members combined, and they always involve women. Before I left for New York three years ago, there was talk of him and a married Hallyu star. *He's even an international flirt.* "It's best we pretend it did not happen."

"Why?" he asks. "Because it was a one-night thing?"

Swallowing hard, I press my lips together before answering him. "No, because I regret that it did."

My eyes meet his. What was that look? Hurt? It can't have been. Our gazes hold. I need him to know I mean my words. Knots form in the pit of my stomach, however, because his look is so intimidating. And there's something about the way he smiles when he looks at me like that. His eyes search mine, then slowly move to my lips and lower.

I suddenly feel self-conscious in the white low-cut blouse I'm wearing and the urge to use the kimono to cover it becomes almost irresistible.

"Don't look at me like that either." *It's unnerving and it reminds me of the reason why I lost my senses last night.*

"Like what?" A chuckle spews from his lips as he leans

closer. "You want me to act like I don't find you attractive? I'm not the kind of man who does that."

"Why? Because it's fun for you to flirt?"

"No, because I *do* find you attractive." His gaze burns mine.

Inhaling sharply, I feel that compliment all the way to my core, a wave of electrifying tingles rushes right through me. Jay and Chase return before I get the chance to reply, and I turn away to face them, plastering on a smile. "So, Amy, how's the Big Apple treating you?"

"Great," I answer with enthusiasm. "At least, I've tried to make the most of my time there."

Chase, Jay, and I talk about my fashion line and my design for the wedding dress. Once or twice, I glance to my side and find Dylan looking openly at me. Why doesn't he try to hide that fact in any way?

THE NEXT DAY, WHEN I MEET WITH MY BROTHER AND Mika by the beach, Dylan is singing to a crowd with his guitar.

"It's a game," Mika whispers to me when I join them at their table. She is beaming as she stares at Dylan again, while I pick a glass and pour myself some wine. His voice is a melodious sound that entraps everyone around us, and it makes me nod to the rhythm of the song.

Chase and Jay are playing the instruments, Lucas stands up from his seat and pulls Mika to her feet so they can both walk to the middle of the stage. I start to cheer as Lucas picks a mic, gets on his knees, and starts singing to Mika.

And when the performance ends, I get on my feet and

cheer loudly, then laugh hard as they all return to their seats. Dylan quickly takes the spot beside mine and drops his guitar on the ground.

"Wasn't that amazing?" he asks me before the others return.

I give him a stiff smile when I look at him, then turn away again. Through the corner of my eye, I catch him shaking his head before he comments. "Stubborn."

There's no way I'll let him know I admire him. Because I can't. *We* can't. Whatever happened that night can never happen again. So, I can't give Dylan any reason to hang on to what transpired between us. Even if he doesn't seem remorseful for what happened at all, and if I'm honest with myself, neither am I. But now that we know who we are, there is no way we can let it happen again. I am too young and naïve. He is too sexy, seasoned, and experienced. We would never work, even if my brother accepted us. A decade of experience makes me feel like a little kid next to an adult who has seen it all. And trust me, as a rockstar play-boy, he probably has. I have never even seen a fully naked guy yet. Like ever.

Our beach outing lasts for a long time. Mika and I start talking about a few changes she has thought about for the dress, and I create a mental picture of what she wants. This is my one chance at proving my skill and I have to make sure everything is perfect.

"We could try out more lace on the sleeves, too," I suggest.

"Yes, I'd like that."

Mika is very easygoing with what she wants and takes advice well. It's hard to work with people who are stuck trying to re-create the image of that perfect style they saw on some model. Fashion, as I see it, is all about highlighting your style and body with perfectly tailored clothes, not changing what fits others to try and make it work for you. My slogan is exactly that. *A one-of-a-kind style for a one-of-a-kind mind.*

"How about light pink for the chief bride's maid?" she asks.

"That might be perfect."

Time flies by as we enjoy our time at the beach, and when Mika leaves with Lucas, Chase and Jay also get up to leave.

"You coming?" they ask Dylan, but he shakes his head immediately.

"I'll hang out with Amy for a while,"

When they leave, I turn to him. "Hang out with Amy?"

"Sure, you're a great company," he replies, then winks at me.

He picks up his glass and sips the wine. "Relax, you're too young to be this grumpy."

"I'm not grumpy," I defend in a tiny voice, and he laughs. "I'm *not.*"

"Of course, you're not, though you really are too young. However, I had fun with you the last time on the beach and that's why I'm staying back."

Our eyes meet. There's a smile on his lips and even though I want to ignore it, I still find it charming. Dylan's looks can steal anyone's breath away. He's wearing his hair in a ponytail today. I find that more attractive than anything else. Oh, and his eyes. His eyes are captivating.

I relax on my chair again and look at the dancers rolling their hips to the music in the background. A memory of our bodies glued to each other's enters my mind and leaves me flushed. And even though nothing more happened, the memory of his touch haunts me. Perhaps Dylan remembers it too because he looks at me again, and this time, there's a familiar tension in the air.

"I really want to act like it didn't happen, though," I say, and my breath hitches in my throat when he extends a hand and strokes my right cheek. My heart quivers, and I subconsciously lean into his touch.

"We should do that," he says in a husky tone. And I can't pull away. "I want to do that too, but ... There's something about the way you look at me, Amy. It makes it impossible not to remember that night."

I nibble on my lower lip, and he leans closer to me, brushing his lips over mine. The contact makes me freeze in my chair, but I instantly miss it as he withdraws from me.

This is crazy, I tell myself. He's so much older, so much more experienced. And he is my brother's best friend. The perfect trifecta for disaster. But another voice in my head tells me to indulge one last time. Everyone on the beach is lost in the dancers' performance. It is windy around us. Noisy, too. I am almost certain he won't hear my heart ramming against my rib cage.

Just this once, I tell myself as I hold the collar of his shirt and stop him from withdrawing completely. "This too never happened," I say, plastering my lips on his and granting permission for his tongue to invade my mouth.

He groans softly, the sound heightens my pleasure and clouds my judgment, and I let the kiss stretch on for a while. His lips are cool over mine, the heat of his breath touches my skin, and when he nibbles on my lower lip, then licks the spot, I moan and tighten my grip on the collar of his shirt.

Dylan suddenly pulls back from me and looks away. He takes off the band on his hair, combs his fingers through his strands, then rubs a hand over his face.

"You're right," he says. "We should pretend it never happened."

"I am right," I murmur, and he nods.

Getting on his feet, he gives me one last look and shakes his head before walking away. My eyes follow him till I can't see his figure anymore. Shutting my eyes, I release a deep breath. *This is what we should do. We have so much against us,* I tell myself, but why did his agreeing to it make me feel a bit sad?

Why does it feel like I will miss and crave more of him soon?

5

———

DYLAN

I just needed to taste her one last time. That is my justification for our kiss on the beach yesterday evening.

Amy is right about her decision to forget about that night. Nothing good can come out of my growing hunger for her, so it is best to bury it. Our age difference and her brother are two giant obstacles we have no way of ever over-coming. Lucas would kill me. And I'm too old for her. But my head and my heart don't see eye-to-eye. And I still dream of her. Of what I want to do with her. To her. How her body would taste and feel around me. How I would take her. Own her.

I wake up early with her on my mind. It's crazy because this is the same little girl I had seen once or twice during the summers I visited Lucas's house for the holidays. Back then, she was a little girl playing around her parents' house on her own, and I remember her being in so much awe of her brother.

Get her out of your head, man. She's too young. Too innocent for you. Easier said than done, though.

I spend my morning writing music and practicing notes for the song. The tour is more important to me now. I plan to launch my foundation while touring, and at every performance, I want to perform a song for the people out there who need hope to keep them living.

I need so much more ... bring me on .... There's a life that's worth living more...

The lyrics flow through my thoughts, but I need to make sure they fit into the tune playing in my head, so I sing them out loud repeatedly.

The ringing of my phone distracts me. I pick it up without checking the caller's ID.

"Dylan, thank God you picked up, I need your help," Mika says on the other end. "Please don't say no."

"I need to know what you want first, Mika," I reply and rub my forehead. My eyes drift to the clock on my wall. It's barely past ten am, and everyone else ought to be out of the hotel already. The days to the wedding are rolling by slowly.

"I know you're busy right now, but Lucas had to drive out with Chase and Jay to get a few last-minute things, and I need to pick my mom up from the airport on my own, so I kind of need help with my dress."

"Your dress?"

Mika sighs. "Just ... Can you come over to my room? I'll explain better when you get here."

"Alright."

"Ugh, you're a lifesaver."

Mika ends the call and I put my guitar aside. Picking a T-shirt from the small corner closet, I put it on before heading out of my room. I love T-shirts and tend to use them to fit my mood. This one says, "Just Say No," which is hilarious because I'm the one who should take this advice. Oh well.

Once I get to Mika's room and knock, she opens immediately.

"Great, I need you to help Amy out with the fitting. She needs help, there's no one else here because I need to hurry out," she explains as she wraps a shawl around her neck, then ties her hair in a bun.

"Wait, Mika..." Mika is out of the door before I can stop her.

I turn to see Amy standing in a corner holding a jar of pins and a hanger of white lace. Her eyes are wide, her cheeks colored a lovely shade of crimson, and I can tell from the crease lines on her forehead that she is stressed.

A small laugh erupts from me before I can stop it.

"Why is it funny?" she asks accusingly.

"It's not ... really, but you need to see the look on your face," I say in-between chuckles. "You look like you're going to explode any minute now."

"You think?" she asks before she moves and drops the lace she's holding on the chair. She raises her hands in the air and stretches, the oversized T-shirt she's wearing rides high on her legs and gives me a good glimpse of the creamy skin of her thighs. My body tightens as I remember trailing my hands up her thighs and close to the apex.

Should I stop? I had asked.

No, not now .... I clear my throat to break the spell the memory created. Amy is the sexiest woman I have ever seen. She has a petite figure, her legs are long and toned, her butt just the perfect size for my hands, and her abs are the perfect mix of hard and soft. My fingers itch to touch her again, and an intense pool of desire erupts through me, nearly stealing my senses away.

"Alright, I'm going to need you to play dummy," she says and spins around to look at me.

I don't hear her at first, but when she walks up to me and shoves the lace she's holding on my chest, I blink back to reality and grab her hands to hold my balance.

"What?"

"I need you to be my mannequin."

My hands are holding hers tight to my chest and we are standing so close to each other I can see the top of her head, but when I lower my eyes, I stare at her full lips and lustful thoughts consume my mind again, making me forget why *we* are a bad idea.

"Oh." I release her abruptly and she steps away, turns again, and moves to pick up the lace.

As I stand in the same spot, she wraps the lace around me. As her hands drift over my body, I feel heat rising inside me. I'm flushed and she knows it because her eyes somehow land on me every minute.

She starts to pin the edges of the lace around me, and I scratch my brow, wondering what she's doing. Her scent intoxicates me and makes me forget the decision I made the previous day. Staying away from Amy should be the only thing on my mind, but here I am, wrapped with white lace like a barbie doll, and the only reason I am not protesting is that I am enjoying the feel of her hands on me too much.

"What are you trying to do?" I ask her after a long time of silence. She makes me straighten my hands out to the side, taking another lace and starting to examine the patterns.

There's a pin in her mouth, and she steps back to look at me fully.

"Don't I look ridiculous?"

"You do, actually," she replies and turns away.

I scoff and watch her go to the dress displayed on the bed. "I think I'm missing something," she murmurs as she examines the dress.

"Just imagine you're a mannequin," she continues when she walks back to me. "I need to get the patterns of this lace so I can cut out the sleeves of the dress and finally sew it all together."

"So, you need to replicate the style of the dress on my body?"

"Exactly," she answers and looks at me. "Ooh, you're smart."

I tilt my head to the right and smile. "Of course, I am. I was a straight As student in high school. Your brother could barely get a word right in his tests."

She laughs, and I see the flash of her adorable dimples. "Lucas could get away with anything because he's my mom's favorite. I came back with anything less than a B and I got grounded so I could study more."

"It's not fair, I know," I reply laughing, and she joins me.

I point at the dress on the bed. "You made that all on your own?"

"Yes, with my friend's help, though. Cassie, she's my assistant and she's ditched me since we got to the island. All I've gotten from her is a text saying, 'Hey Amy, I know you want to kill me, but I'll explain it all once I get back'.... I think she ditched me for some guy."

I laugh. "He must be handsome, then."

Amy shrugs and comes close to my side. She layers out the lace and pins it together.

"Do you think this pattern works well for the sleeves? Should I make it a blend? Like something with glitters and shiny stones on plain net instead of this same lace?"

I look at the lace in my hand. "I think the first one sounds better ... More unique."

She folds her hands over her chest. "I think so too."

She starts to take the pins off my body and once she's done, I can finally move. There's a little cramp in my shoulder muscles but it doesn't matter, because even though I know I shouldn't, I'm glad that I'm here with her.

I follow her to the bed when she walks away, and we look at the dress together. Amy is a talented designer. I can tell she paid attention to detail as she made this dress. I imagine Mika in it and know it will fit her perfectly.

"This is a brilliant job," I say to her.

"You think so?"

I nod. "It looks like it was made just for Mika and that sleeve idea you came up with would make it a killer."

Amy grins. "That's so relieving to hear. I've spent hours wondering if I should ruin it all and start afresh. Mika would have my neck, but I just want it to be perfect."

"You're quite the perfectionist, aren't you?"

It takes a while before she answers. "Not at all ... I know there should always be room for mistakes, but this is my break-out design and that means I don't have the luxury to make any. People all over the States and the world will watch Lucas's very public island-themed wedding and will wonder who made this dress. Keaton Designs needs to be remembered after that day."

She looks at me then, and a soft smile plays on her lips. "You might think it's crazy, but it's my dream."

"Actually, I don't think that's crazy at all," I tell her, then flop on the bed. "I dream of something similar."

"Really?" she sits beside me and folds her legs on the bed. "What's that?"

It's my first time discussing myself with a woman like

this. Most times, we talk about the basics while our chemistry builds, and after that it never gets personal. I like to keep my thoughts to myself. But sharing them with Amy does not feel like an intrusion at all.

Instead, it feels natural to talk to her like this.

"I want people to listen to my songs and feel inspired. No one besides my guys and manager knows this, but on our upcoming tour, I plan to launch a foundation that will inspire people dealing with the trauma of domestic violence."

"Why domestic violence?" she asks in a tender voice. The softness is like a trap that lures me in, and I find myself leaning closer to her.

I get lost in her eyes for a second, but instead of saying more, I shrug.

"I find it a worthy cause and they need help, I guess."

A part of me wants to share more with her, but the way my heartbeat races stops me. I never feel this urge with anyone, and every part of me wants to fight it off. Holding back personal bits of myself is never a problem with anyone, but this woman's eyes somehow make me feel like I can indulge in the comfort they offer. She is not a woman, She is a girl. *A much, much younger girl, and you need to remember that.*

Besides, it *never ends well.* My father is a brilliant example. I spent my childhood watching him suffer because he trusted the wrong woman. And that *will never happen to me.*

I look at Amy again and she gives me a soft smile, then nods. "They do need inspiring, and your voice is soothing enough."

She swings her legs down and props her hands behind her on the bed.

My chest becomes heavy and the flutters in the pit of my stomach become much more intense. It makes me breathless, and hot, so I stand up and clap my hands together to lighten the mood. "How about we order room service before you continue? I'm famished."

"I'll take whatever seafood they have."

6

———

AMY

I'm having dinner with my mom, Lucas, and Mika the next evening, and when I join them at the hotel restaurant, it is almost seven pm. It is also the first time I'm seeing my mother in a long time. She looks the same to me. Her smile is as brilliant as ever, her hair the same dirty shade of blonde as mine, and as usual, she is doting on Lucas.

"Oh, you get bigger each time I see you," she states, as if he is a little child.

"Hey Mom," I greet, then lean down to kiss her on both cheeks before hugging her a little. "You look amazing."

"Oh, you do too, Amy dear," she replies. "I love your outfit. You made this?"

"Yes."

My mother is always painfully honest with her opinions, and I'm expecting a comment on the style of my satin dress or the quality of its design, but she simply looks at me again and claps her hands together. "OMG, I love it."

After sitting, I link my fingers and place my hands on the table in front of me. The weather is cooler than usual outside. The wedding is only a few days away, and I wonder how Mika is feeling at this point.

Mika looks at ease as she talks to my mother. They both get along fine, and I suspect Lucas is a great impact on that relationship because my mom is quite picky with friends. Even though I know she isn't judgmental, she comes off that way sometimes.

"How has it been in New York? I was reading a magazine recently, and it mentioned Keaton Designs. I was so proud my baby girl got into fine print, and I can't wait to see what you've come up with for the wedding dress," my mother says as she reaches out to touch my hand a little.

"Amy's going to do great, I'm sure," Lucas answers for me. "I got a glimpse of what she's working on already, and Mika also loves it."

"It's amazing, I can't wait for everyone else to see it," Mika comments. "I'm sure I'll turn heads."

I join in the laughter at the table, and a waiter returns with our bottle of wine and some ice. After ordering some baked French fries and steak, I look at my mom again.

"How's it going with the company?" I ask.

After my father's death, she began handling the full operations of our family's real estate business. Lucas was more focused on his music career and I preferred fashion designing, so she had to take on the responsibility on her own. She sold part of it to be able to invest in Lucas, of course, but she still kept the majority of the shares.

"As best as I can," she answers. "I always thought I'd get help from one of you guys, but turns out you prefer playing dress-up, and Lucas here loves being famous."

"It's more than playing dress-up, Mom," I interrupt.

"It's not just about the fame either," Lucas says.

She looks from me to Lucas, then she chuckles. "Of course, it's not," she says. "One of you will have to take over at some point, though." She looks at me then and I know she is solely referring to me. "You were always so good at marketing, and your father always believed his little girl would take after him."

I clear my throat because the moment becomes tense, and I lift my wine glass to my lips. After sipping, I rub the back of my neck a little and sigh. My mother's issue with my choice of career exists because she had different expectations. I want to be my own woman, and she simply wishes I would follow in my father's footsteps, or better still, my brother's.

"You have such beautiful talent, Amy, and you're good with people ... Why hide behind a layer of clothes and spend your time with needles and fabrics?"

I'm about to respond when the waiter returns with two others carrying trays of our meal.

"This is my dinner and it's my wedding week," Lucas says then, as he lifts his wine glass. "We should toast, eat, and wear our biggest smiles to celebrate my lifelong commitment to the woman of my dreams."

My mother's lips curve into a warm smile again. The corners of her eyes crinkle, and I watch her shift her entire attention to Lucas. "To my baby, Lucas, and his lovely wife, Mika."

"To love and friendship," Lucas adds, then clinks his glass to hers, then on Mika's before mine.

I push down every worrisome thought spearing up inside me because of my mother's comment, and I toast with Lucas. "To love and friendship."

The rest of dinner goes on smoothly, but I start wishing I was somewhere else. Perhaps standing by the beach, enjoying the night's cool air, or listening to the melodious sound of Dylan's voice as he sings to a crowd.

Warmth flushes my skin when I remember the intensity of his eyes each time he stares at me. My breath hitches in my throat in response, and I sip from my wine, hoping the fiery feel of the alcohol burns away the tingles inside me. This line of thought will get me nowhere, except to disappointment and hurt. A forbidden affair that would never amount to anything more.

I blink back to reality and join in the conversation before anyone notices. I know Dylan is not a man I should think about, but I still can't help myself as each time he enters my thoughts, a tingling sensation creeps up to my heart, and I love it and hate it in equal measures.

THE BOAT CRUISE WAS CHASE'S SUGGESTION FOR THE next afternoon's event. The guy is a romantic. His navy-blue eyes were shining as he told us what we would be doing. I remember hearing him mentioning once that he will live his life to the fullest, until he meets *the one*, because, as with his parents, he plans on only marrying once and for life.

I stand on the dockside alone after we finish a game of cards inside, and I'm enjoying the view of the perfect ocean.

My hands are crossed over my chest, and the wind blows my hair and kimono away, but I don't mind. I enjoy the feel of the wind on my skin and the tickles in my nostrils whenever I inhale the scent of sea salt in the air.

Standing here, the notion of time vanishes, and my mind is far away, focused on my life. Once the wedding is over, I plan on returning to New York for preparations.

With the publicity I aim to get here, I'm certain I will land a chance to showcase my style at the upcoming New York Fashion Week. And after that, perhaps Paris Fashion Week too. That is the dream, at least, and I have a feeling I am about to reach new heights.

"You seem lost in thought." The deep voice causes me to turn and there stands Dylan, his right hand in the pocket of his shorts, and his T-shirt molding to his muscles. My eyes drift down his chest

and my fingers itch to touch him. A vivid image of my fingers trailing down to his abdomen flashes in my mind. Heat floods the back of my neck and my cheeks, and I'm certain there's a crimson color visible there because he grins at me and closes the rest of the distance between us.

"I wasn't," I reply and clear my throat a bit, so I don't sound husky. "I was just enjoying the view."

Dylan stands beside me, then leans on the rails with both hands. "Wait till the sun sets, that's when you'll see the real beauty. There's always this glitter in the sun's dying shine, and the orange hints on the horizon are what I love best."

He angles his head to look at me and I'm lost in his eyes. "You watch it often?" I ask and move closer to him without even realizing what I'm doing. As forbidden as he is to me, he is like the sun. There's a magnetic pull I can't resist, and my muscles shiver from the slow, climbing desire that buds inside of me.

"I do," he answers. "My most creative time is when I'm alone watching the sunset or admiring any form of nature."

"Oh … That's lovely," I whisper. My heart starts pounding in my chest when he gives me a small smile, and I gasp when he lifts his right hand and brushes it over my cheeks. He puts some strands of my hair behind my ears and cups my chin. "Where are the others?" I ask in a shaky voice. The roaring of my pulse blocks out every other sound, and I wonder if Dylan can hear too.

"Playing a board game inside," he answers as he inches closer. "This shouldn't happen."

"I know." My chest swells, and I inhaled sharply when his thumb moves to my lower lip. "This never happened."

All thought and reason flea me as my lids flutter closed just as he tastes me. His warm tongue sweeps over the roof of my mouth as I part for him so I meet his kiss with fervent passion. My hands are at my sides, and I lift them, wrap them around his neck, and press closer to him.

Everything else seizes to exist. Dylan's scent consumes my mind. I'm lost in his embrace, the skill of his lips and tongue moving over mine, and the flutters consuming my chest.

I hear a clang, and we spring apart with force. I nearly miss a step, but I steady myself by grabbing the railing and I turn to see Mika standing opposite us, a shocked look on her face.

"I'm sorry. I was ... Dylan was ..." she stammers, then turns around and hurries away.

I groan, close my eyes, and comb my fingers through my hair. Dylan is quiet and even when I open my eyes he is staring at me. "I should talk to Mika," I say instantly feeling guilt. "If she tells Lucas ...."

"Are you that scared of your brother's reaction?" he asks.

"What? This isn't just about Lucas."

"Then what is this about? I'm not that sorry for kissing you, Amy."

My heart thunders in my chest because of his last statement. Because I'm not that sorry either. I nearly lose control and fling myself in his arms so I can feel the warmth of his skilled lips again. I touch the back of my neck, rub it, and move my hand to my cheeks before I touch my lower lip lightly. But reality wins out.

"You know why this is a bad idea," I reply. "You're Dylan … You're …" I trail off, sigh, and shut my eyes. My body wants him, my heart keeps pounding, and none of this makes any sense.

Without another word to him, I hurry along to find Mika. She's sitting alone inside a room on the middle deck, and she's staring at her phone screen. "Mika," I call, and she turns to me before I join her on the couch.

A smile forms on my lips when I notice she is staring at a group picture of Lucas and the other guys. Mika grins at me, and even though I know she is dying to ask me questions, she doesn't.

"Lucas doesn't know," I tell her in a soft voice anyway. "And he shouldn't because there's nothing between us."

Mika is quiet for a while before she asks, "You sure about that?"

No, I'm not. Every time I'm with Dylan I get confused and I forget why I should stay away. "I'm sure," I tell Mika and put my hand on hers. "It's your wedding in two days, now let's get the plans for your bachelorette rolling."

We both laugh as I drag her to her feet, and we hurry out to go find Lucas, Jay, and Chase.

That evening, while we play games and drink on the boat, Dylan is nowhere in sight, and my traitorous mind wanders to him all the time.

7

DYLAN

"I want to be your star and your everything ... Come to me ... Oh, make me crave your kiss," I'm doing back vocals while I play my guitar and I can tell I have the crowd mesmerized.

Lucas is beside me with the mic, and he's letting it all out.

Our singing at the beach bar attracts more people to the stand, and the owner rewards us with another round of free booze when we return to our seats.

"It's your bachelor's night and we shouldn't spend so much time in one place," Jay suggests when we sit down again. I pick up my bottle of beer and take a long swing from it.

"Where do you suggest we go next?" Lucas asks.

We started the night at a five-star restaurant in Maui's main town, and after that, we went shopping for rings because Lucas forgot to buy them earlier.

"I heard about this club downtown. It's supposed to be really in right now and it would be the best way to end the night," Chase suggests. But, as per usual, I'm in no mood for loud music and dancing.

Unlike Jay, who adds, "Yes, that's definitely the best way to end the night. Besides, it's your last night a free man, bro, you need to wild it all up tonight." Always ready for nightlife and a good time, these two. And they say *I'm* the playboy. These two are each other's wingmen and they hardly ever spend a night on their own. They love this life and though I know a few things about their pasts, I know they are doing all they can to enjoy life to the fullest.

I love my soul brothers, and I can't even imagine my life without them.

They continue talking, and having decided the night ends here for me, I tune them out. Looking around, I spot a middle-aged couple at the far end speaking heatedly to each other. The man gets up to leave, but the woman grabs his wrists and pulls him back down.

The scene stirs a dull ache inside me, and I avert my eyes immediately.

"You coming with us, D?" Chase asks when they start gathering their items on the table.

"I ... Uh ... need to practice for the song for the reception tomorrow," I lie.

My friends never push when I decline an offer to hang out with them. I'm the group's loner, and even though they mostly think I prefer spending my time with women when I'm not with them, truth is, I just rather be on my own.

"Meeting up with Louisa tonight? Or Anna?" Lucas asks.

"Maybe he is meeting both." Jay says.

"What? They're not even on the island."

They laugh at my reply and Lucas pats my shoulder. "We're kidding, man. See you later."

When they all leave, I grab the last bottle, pop it open with the rings on my finger, and drink from it, deeply. My eyes drift to the couple I spotted earlier again, and I notice the woman is still nagging.

Watching the scene reminds me of my mother, and I hate the prickly sensation that creeps through me. Growing annoyed, I get on my feet, pick up my guitar bag, and sling it over my shoulder before walking away.

The stroll back to the hotel is a long one. I take off my Italian slides and hold them so I can feel the damp sand under my feet. I wonder if my mother ever regretted the way she treated my dad and me in the past.

I last saw her fifteen years ago, and not once has she tried to reach out to me.

My dad and I keep in touch frequently, he remains a big fan of our band, and once or twice after the shows, he calls to congratulate me. Speaking to him is always a source of comfort, and strangely, I feel the urge to hear his voice tonight.

I take my phone out when the hotel comes into view and dial his number. He doesn't pick up after three rings, so I give up. I'll call again later. When I get to the front of the hotel, a delivery bike is parked out front, and Amy walks out of the building wearing shorts and a baggy t-shirt. Her hair is a mess, there's a pen in between her lips, and my best guess is she has been working.

She doesn't see me at first, till the biker rides off. Her head turns in my direction and a grin breaks out on my lips before I can stop it. There's just that warmth and lightness that spreads through my heart when I see her, and frankly, she is the first woman to ever make me wonder about her. Forbidden or not, I feel like this is something I would really like to experience. Even if for a little while, because I know well and truly that nothing lasting will come from this fascination of mine.

"Hey," I say when I walk to her.

"Hi," she replies.

"I'd love to join you," I tell her, and she shrugs as we walk into the hotel together. "You're not at the bachelorette?"

"I was," she answers. "But Mika had too much to drink, so we ended it early."

I glance at my watch and realize it's only past eleven. "I'm sure my guys won't be back till dawn."

"They sure love to party hard," she says as she laughs. "Why aren't you with them?"

"I'm not much of a partier," I answer.

She arches a brow and gives me a suspicious look that's funny to me. "Why do I find that hard to believe? I mean, the shirt you have on right now says, 'Party hard or Die'."

"You can't judge me by my clothes, come on," I reply.

She pulls her room door open, and we both enter before she locks it and drops the box of pizza on the bed. She puts her hands on her waist and continues in an amused tone. "The other day, you had a 'Crazy bitches love me' shirt on. That first night at the bar, it was an 'At my funeral, take a bouquet from my coffin and throw it to the crowd to see who's next'. Your style screams bad-boy Rockstar every time."

"I didn't know you noticed those little things."

"It's hard not to," she replies before a burst of riotous laughter leaves her lips. A surge of adrenaline courses through me and makes my breath hitch in my throat.

In that moment, Amy is the most beautiful woman I have ever seen.

THERE ARE MANY REASONS WHY I SHOULD STAY AWAY from her, but I can't think of any as I stare into her eyes. Amy's mesmerizing, and there's something seductive about her breathless laugh.

"Maybe I'll wear my "What's wrong with you people?" shirt for the wedding tomorrow. You seem to think I'm a controversial lover."

"But you are," she answers again in that light voice. I scoff and allow my eyes to drift over her body, while she continues, "You're quite popular with the ladies too. If it was your wedding, I'm sure it'd be a shock to the entire country."

"Are you saying you don't think I can fall in love and marry?"

Amy pauses and looks at me intently, "You just don't seem like the type," she replies.

She isn't wrong about that, though. Her analysis makes me wonder if she is the type of woman who wants flowers and a knight to sweep her off her feet with romance.

"What about you? Planning to have a bunch of kids somewhere someday?"

"A family, yes, at some point. I mean, who doesn't want to have one?"

Her eyes cling to mine, and I don't need to say anything at that point because the smile on her lips withers. "You don't."

I lift my left shoulder nonchalantly. "It's not important to me. Not everyone experiences happily ever afters or believes in them. I believe in passion, and that fades away with time."

Just like what I'm feeling for her right now. If I take her now, I might be able to rid myself of this desire. *Maybe my heart will stop pounding when she is close, or when we are alone.*

"Not all passion fades," she says as she puts a hand on her neck. I see her chest rise and fall when she takes a deep breath.

The air around us tenses. She notices too because she stops laughing and presses a hand over her chest. I can get to her with two strides and everything else will be history. If I take her now, I'm scared I will never stop craving her.

I still dream of our night together. Never has a woman made it into my dreams.

Our physical relationships stayed that way—physical, but this ... This attraction seems explosive. Amy is different, I can sense it. Not only has she been haunting my thoughts, and we haven't even had sex yet, I want to know more about her, I think I can sit and listen to the sound of her laughing the entire day.

A line from the song I intend to sing at the reception tomorrow enters my mind. *The smile in your eyes is all I want to hear.* I find myself relating to those lyrics more than anything else.

Neither of us moves for a second, but in the next moment, she is in my arms and my lips are on hers. Just like I imagined, it is explosive, and the heat tunneling through me burns.

My hands move down her back and under her shirt, her skin is cool, her waist small, and when she moans, I forget everything else, deepen the kiss, and lift her off the ground so her legs wrap around my waist.

"Dylan," she gasps when I drag my lips to her neck.

"Don't think," I whisper. "I don't want to think."

The reasoning would make it impossible for me to take

what I want in this moment. Amy's body wrapped passionately against mine is the only thing I need for the night.

I carry her to the bed, her pizza lies forgotten, and my fingers find the button of her shorts. She moans when I push them down her legs, my lips feast on hers again before they move to the pulse at the side of her neck. Every neuron in my body fires, I want to savor the sweetness of her body as I remember it, but I also want to make her shiver till she cries out my name.

This is insane. This is amazing.

The feelings she invokes in me are like an awakening. I have never wanted anyone like this before. My lips kiss every inch of her skin. She cries out when I cover her nipples with my mouth and lift her off the bed, so her body presses harder against mine.

"I need you, Amy," I whisper into her ear, and she shudders beneath me. The hum of desire in my blood ravages through my veins till I can no longer deny it the chance to manifest.

Our fingers cross and I hold on tight as I kiss down to her abdomen and stop just inches above the apex of her thighs. Her thighs part for me, and I pleasure her with my tongue, loving the sounds of her breathless gasps and whimpers of pleasure. She is so responsive.

It's like her body is made for my pleasure, and I want to indulge for as long as I can. Her hands glide down my chest when I release her. Her touch makes me melt inside, our eyes meet and the heat in her stare is enough to scorch me into kissing her again.

My fingers move into her hair, I pull her closer with my other hand around her waist and I push into her slowly, wanting to feel the warmth of her core wrapped around me. She is so tight. So tight, but she takes me to the hilt.

A groan escapes my lips, and I hold still when I am inside her fully. Her breathing is hard and her eyes are close shut. We stay like that as I let her adjust to my size. Until she rocks her hips into mine. And just like that, I'm lost. My thrusts start slow and deep, and she responds with passion, gasping with each stroke and moaning with each pull.

Her teeth nibble on her lower lip, the image of her hair spread over the pillows and her skin so white under the fluorescent bulb ingrains in my memory.

"You're perfect," I murmur, wanting her to know just what she does to me.

Our sleek movements are not just passionate, we are fire. It's the best moment I have ever experienced with anyone. It's everything to me.

She's small in my hands, her creamy skin is hot under my touch, or maybe it's my own body heat. I can't tell. Amy's body squeezes mine and draws a deep growl from my lips. My hips move faster, and my lips find her erect nipples again.

She meets my thrusts eagerly, and I want to give her more pleasure, so I trail my right hand down her body to the soft nub of her clit. Amy climaxes against me. Hard. Her body milks mine till I can't hold back, and I follow her over the edge while her nails dig into my right arm.

It takes a long time for our harsh breathing to return to normal, but when I raise my head to look at her, my heart still stutters in my chest.

Oh boy!

Amy's lips are slightly parted and swollen, her cheeks are a lovely pink shade, and when she exhales, her hot breath touches my face. My body is still buried inside her, and it stirs again.

Slowly, she lifts a hand to my cheeks and slips her

fingers into my hair to pull my head down. I let her kiss me, and I move inside her again. *It's just one night,* I tell myself. I'm certain that by the end of our stay on the island, this chemistry with Amy will be gone, just like with the other women I have been with.

8

———

AMY

Dylan doesn't know it but he was my first. I thought for sure it would happen that night at the beach, but we fell asleep as soon as our heads touched those pillows. It was my only regret at the time, but I have no regrets now. He is a passionate lover, attentive and gentle, and he plays my body like it's the strings of his guitar. I couldn't bring myself to tell him I was a virgin, but even without knowing, he made sure I was okay before he started moving inside me. It was perfect and I wouldn't mind seeing if this morning it still feels the same. It's why, when I wake up the next morning and don't find him in bed beside me, my heart sinks a little.

What have I done? Last night was magical. Nothing has ever felt better. I didn't even know something could feel like that. And now, my heart is full of him. I cover my face with my hands, close my eyes and sigh. His scent still clings to the bedsheets, and I lay back down for a second to indulge a little.

Knots form in the pit of my stomach, and a tingle races up my spine. *What were you thinking, Amy? You know better.* A grin appears on my face regardless of the voice in my head warning me not to feel. How can I not? There's a languid pool of ecstasy still coursing through my veins.

Dylan is all I can think about.

A rapt knock on my door makes me jump out of bed. My eyes land on the wall clock. It's past seven am, and I groan. *Shoot.* It's Lucas's wedding!

I slip into my shorts and shirt and hurry to the door. Chase is standing on the other side, with a frown on his face. He combs his fingers through his blond hair and fixes his blue eyes on mine. "I can't find Mika anywhere."

"What? I don't understand, she's in her room."

"No, she's not. Lucas is freaking out ... He went to check on her, and she wasn't there, so he went around the hotel while trying her number and she's nowhere around here. The guys are all searching for her. You're the only one not up yet and I thought she might be with you."

My hand covers my lips. "She's not," I stammer.

I follow Chase after closing my room door, and when we get outside, Jay and Lucas are in front of the hotel, and Dylan comes from the side of the building to join us. He doesn't look at me, but I immediately can't take my eyes off him.

My hands are in the back pockets of my jeans short, and just the sight of him makes me tingle all over. His forehead is creased with fine worry lines, and he is saying something to Jay and Lucas that I can't hear because I'm too busy lusting over him.

He makes a small hand gesture, and I remember his hands moving down my body and going around my neck.

"I'll check the town's market. Sometimes, she likes strolling past shops and buying stuff she doesn't need," Lucas says.

"I'll check the beach side," I suggest. "Dylan can come with me; we'll cover more grounds if we're two."

"That sounds like a plan," Chase agrees audibly before anyone else can protest.

I wait till they all leave and walk over to Dylan, placing a hand on his arm. "Let's check the beach."

Dylan looks at me, then gives me a wavering smile. For a moment, I'm scared he will pull away, but I relax a little when he doesn't. We walk in silence till we get to the beach, and from a distance, I see Mika standing alone, facing the ocean.

"I should go talk to her," I say to Dylan. He nods, takes out his phone, and turns away to call Lucas while I hurry toward Mika. When Mika sees me, she smiles a little and I see tears in her eyes. "Mika," I call in a low voice, then close the distance between us and wrap my hands around her. "You scared everyone."

"I didn't mean to do that, I just … Waking up this morning made me realize how real the day is, and I just got too emotional." She smiles and wipes her cheeks with both hands.

She smiles and wipes her cheeks with both hands. "Lucas is so freaked out. You need to see the pale look on his face."

"I'm so sorry," she says in a broken voice, and another fresh wave of tears shines in her eyes. "I'm not having second thoughts or anything, I just needed to be alone for a while to let out these tears … I think they are tears of joy."

She laughs, and I hug her again. "You have me by your side, so you shouldn't worry too much… Today's going to be perfect."

When I glance over my shoulder again, I see Dylan still standing on the same spot, with his hands buried deep in his pockets. The wind blows against his hair. He doesn't move or look away as he stares, and I wonder what's going through his mind.

We return to the hotel some minutes later, and Lucas is waiting outside for us with Chase and Jay. Mika and Lucas immediately get into a hug, and the look of relief on Lucas's face as he hugs her is clear for anyone to see.

"They look good together," I comment as I stand beside Dylan. He angles his head so he can look at me and I smile. "Don't they?" I ask, wanting to know what he thinks and what that expression on his face means.

"They do," Dylan replies. His gaze turns intense, and I shiver because my insides suddenly heat up and the flush rushes through the rest of me. I'm sure the color on my cheeks is obvious, so I plaster my hands on my cheek and blow out air from my lips.

Dylan notices my blush and the corners of his lips curve up a little. Placing his hand on my forehead, he rubs it play-fully before brushing his hand over my hair. I notice Jay and Chase looking at us from the corner of my eye, and I imme-diately step back.

Dylan withdraws quickly too and clears his throat. "Since everything is set, we should do the same, right?" he asks.

Chase is the first to agree, while Mika and Lucas continue to hold hands and grin at each other.

"How bad would it look if we kept the bride and groom waiting? We can't do that to them," Jay replies.

"Then let's get it moving," I announce in a cheery tone.

With everyone heading inside, I follow Mika to her

room to help her get ready. After showering, she sits in front of a wide mirror, and I take out my make-up items to get her set.

Thirty minutes pass filled with laughter and chatter about my brother and his friends while we get her set for her big day. When she slips into her dress, I'm astonished because even though I am the sole designer of the dress, Mika's slender figure and creamy skin just bring it alive.

"You're my first muse," I tell her. "I have worked on countless fashion pieces with mannequins, but this is my first bridal piece on a real human, and it's..."

"Amazing," someone says from the doorway. Mika and I both turn to Dylan who is standing there. He leans against the frame and folds his arms across his chest. "Perfect is what I'll call it. No one else would have done a better job of making Mika look this pretty."

"You flatter me," Mika says as she laughs. She smacks Dylan on the arm playfully when he gets to where she stands, smiles, and touches her cheeks lightly.

"I mean it, you're the most beautiful bride I've ever seen. It makes me wonder if all brides tend to look like this on that special day."

Mika laughs harder, and I excuse myself to go get ready. Mika's beach wedding is going to be top news in the entertainment industry for the next few weeks, and this is just the kind of media coverage I need.

Excited for the day to unfold, I style my hair with pins into a messy bun with a lovely flower attached to the side, then slip into my navy-blue sequined bridal dress.

When I join Mika in her room again, Dylan is still there. Chase and Jay are there too.

"Woah ... Is that Amy?" Chase asks.

"Dude, you're hot," Jay tells me.

"You look amazing, Amy," Mika squeals. Their compliments come at once, making me a bit self-conscious. I slide a hand down the bodice of my dress and suck in a deep breath. Dylan is staring at me, and once again, he has that serious expression on.

I can't read it fully, but one thing is clear. The passion in his intense stare. And it reminds me of our night together. I feel the need to exhale because of the pressure building inside my chest as I remember the gentle strokes of his fingers over my skin and how his breath merged with mine, making me tremble and crave more of him.

"We should get started," Jay announces, walking forward first and extending a hand to me. "May I have the honor of accompanying you, my lady?" he asks, giving me a cheeky smile and a playful bow that makes me laugh.

We head out and to the back of the hotel where Mika's wedding planner already has everything set. Lucas and my mom are talking when we reach them, and the second Lucas sees Mika, he stops what he is saying, and smiles wide at her.

Watching Lucas and Mika together, I wonder if I will ever get to feel that kind of connection and love with anyone. Most times, when I think of relationships, the first thing that comes to mind is my dedication to my work, and my need to focus on that alone.

Dedicating time and knowledge to building my brand is important, but what would it feel like to also have someone close enough to share the small and big wins with? To support me through the rough times. To hold my hand and help me navigate the murky waters of life.

My mother looks pleased as she watches Lucas and Mika throughout the entire event. I'm sitting in the front row as the maid of honor and as they recite their vows, somehow, my eyes wander to the side, and I see Dylan also watching the couple.

His lips are parted in a smile, I see him cheer and laugh as everyone applauds Mika and Lucas after they read their vows, and he also turns to his side and looks my way. Just like that, everything else seizes to exist, and it's just him and me, and I wish it could stay that way.

If only this was meant to be. Does he wonder too?

9
___

DYLAN

It will fade. These three words have become my mantra every time I look at Amy, and my pulse skips a bit. She easily steals my attention even when she is not aware. And being unable to tear my eyes away from her during the wedding was one thing, but the need to touch her tunneling through me is another. *She is forbidden.*

Amy is dancing with Jay now. She laughs and the sound reaches my ears. She glances over her shoulder and picks a glass from the server's tray to sip. When she staggers a bit, I move without thinking and lurch toward her with the intent of catching her, but Jay is close, and his hands slide around her waist.

Seeing him touch her like that, even though he releases her immediately, makes my blood boil. I don't want anyone else touching her ... My muscles are tense just from thinking about it, and I feel the urge to walk over and take her in my arms. I want to be the one dancing with her, so I can stare into those eyes that easily make me forget everything I have believed to be right.

What is this feeling?

It is unsettling, and it makes me hot. Adjusting my tie so I can breathe properly, I can only hope this will ease the tightness in my chest. It doesn't, so I drop the wine glass I'm holding, and I walk over to her.

The fast music playing suddenly turns into a slow one. I notice Lucas's mom and some others lure Mika and Lucas to the red carpet in the middle of the set-up so they can dance, and I ask Amy for a dance too.

She puts her hand in mine, and we start moving to the beat. When I twirl her around and bring her close again, she steps closer to me, and our bodies touch. The spiral of desire that races through me is shocking. Just last night, I had her, and now it is like I cannot get enough of her.

Amy is slowly making her way into my core. This never happens with any woman.

She looks at me and asks. "No smart quote today? I feel like I'm missing out."

I laugh and shake my head before letting my gaze trail down her body. The dress she is wearing is lovely, curve-hugging, and it makes my blood boil hotter. "You look really nice," I compliment as I admire her again. I lower my head a bit and add. "I dare say you've turned a bunch of rags into yet another magnificent dress."

The blush on her face is visible and it fills me with warmth.

We continue dancing for a while, and everything else melts away. It is just two of us now, listening to the song as we glide over the dance floor. Our eyes merge, our breaths mingle, the rise and fall of our chests become one and the connection is extremely different from what I ever felt with anyone.

The song slowly comes to a halt, and we stop moving, but we are still standing there, lost in each other's arms. She licks her lower lip. Lifting a hand, I brush my fingers over her lips. Her eyes close, and I'm lost in the spell that is her.

I nearly dip my head to kiss her, forgetting about everything else, but the applause that suddenly erupts around us breaks that trance.

Looking around, they are cheering at us. Lucas is smiling, but there is a look of confusion there. Mika wears a knowing look, however, and I realize I am still holding Amy's hand when I feel warmth spread from it through the rest of my body.

Not wanting to let her go yet, I stroke the front of her palm with my thumb, and she looks at me again before I gently release her hand. Amy walks away from me and picks a wine glass on her way, I do the same, but head toward Lucas and Mika to congratulate them because nothing good will come from me following Amy.

Soon, it's time for the band to sing for the reception. Lucas takes the mic. Sitting with my guitar, I adjust the mic in front of me also. Lucas points at Mika and starts singing. He grabs the mic after the intro and gives me the chance to play the bridge with my guitar before he continues.

Joining him, I let the lyrics flow through me as I sing out my heart.

I was never mistaken till you, but now that it's over, it's just begun.

Amy is sitting in the second row beside her mother. While her mother is clapping and moving her head along to the rhythm of our song, Amy is sitting there with a pale look on her face, and it makes me wonder what thoughts are going through her head.

Mika joins us on the stage when Lucas gets on his knees and calls her out, we finish the song, and I sing a solo for the couple before leaving the stage for Jay and Chase to play an instrumental melody.

Sitting beside Amy again when no one is looking, I'm caught by the flush on her cheeks when she glances in my direction.

"Dylan," she whispers.

"Amy…."

Her hand is on her lap, and without weighing my actions, I pick it up and link our fingers to test out my response to her. Once again, my heart flutters, and there's this peaceful feeling that swamps me.

"We shouldn't," she says.

"Let's go on a date," I reply. I'm tired of fighting this. Tired of the reasons that keep us apart when all I want is to be close to her. Her eyes widen, and I look at her. "This is Hawaii, there's no reason we can't go on a date in Hawaii and enjoy ourselves."

She smiles and gives me a soft nod. "A date," she whispers, and I nod back.

"A date."

Releasing her hand, I walk away to join my friends. The rest of the evening is light-hearted, and I play the guitar more times than I can remember. Nothing else gives me as much joy as music. It is always my escape route, but it's starting to feel like Amy could easily be my comfort zone.

Why?

Because I don't only want her physically. I want to be close to her, I want to hear her laugh and talk. I want to watch her work, and I want to make love to her even though I already have. As a man who never lets himself get attached to any woman, that's enough reason for me to know Amy is slowly finding her way into my heart.

FOR OUR DATE, I BOOK A TOUR WITH JACK HARTER helicopters to see the parts of Kauai inaccessible by foot. Amy wears a light-blue tank top with mid-thigh jean shorts. I catch myself admiring her lean legs quite too often, and sometimes she catches me staring.

We get to the helicopter hangar after eating breakfast in a nearby restaurant. Mika and Lucas have not yet come out of their bedroom since last night's party, and Jay has plans with Chase to explore the North Beach.

"It feels like a cool day," Amy comments as she adjusts the hat on her hair. Smiling at her, I take it off before she can stop me.

"This looks better on me than on you," I tease as she struggles to get the hat from me, but she is a bit too short, and she needs to stretch before her hand gets to my head, so I have a better advantage at evading her.

She laughs, and putting a hand around her shoulder, I give the hat back. "You should wear your shades to keep the sun rays away from your eyes," I advise.

She grins and adjusts the hat. "Don't tell me what to do, old man." Amy pokes my side. I groan, and she breaks free from me. We continue playing like that till the helicopter finally reaches the ground.

I take her hand and hear her gasp when I link our fingers. "Come on," I say and lead her toward the helicopter. Sitting by the window, Amy stares outside the entire time.

"Want to know something impressive?" I ask her and she turns to me.

"Yeah..."

"I can fly the damn thing," I replied. "The helicopter."

"What?" she asks, the word a long drawl on her lips. "That's insane, where did you learn?"

I shrug. "The pilot is my friend," I reply. "I take one or two lessons when I have time, and my dad was a pilot too."

"Was?" she asks.

"Yeah, was ..." Answering her question makes me remember him, and what our life was like when I was younger. He never had time for anything else besides his job, and that made my mother very bitter for many years.

When he eventually stopped working, I thought it would make my mother happier, but it only worsened. She nagged at everything, cursed and swore at anything, especially when she had too much to drink.

Most times, she brought home a bottle or two, so she could spend the night ranting and drowning her sorrows. My father never said anything to her or argued with her. It made me wonder what kind of person he was.

Too easygoing and let himself get hurt. I can't ever let that happen to me.

"My father died when I was very little," Amy said. "He worked on marketing but had a dream of being a fashionista himself. Thinking of feeding his family more than his dream, he gave up his chosen career to build our family company. He had actually started working on fashion before he married my mother but his brand never made it far. After he passed, my mother took over the company and sold off a chunk of shares so she could start something more beneficial, in her own words."

"Beneficial?" I ask and Amy nods.

A smile forms on her lips, but I notice the sadness in her eyes. "Soul Sounds," she continues, mentioning the name of our band. "Lucas was talent to her, and she made him into the star he is. She used all the money she could afford to invest in the band and get a magnificent manager like Ken Daystar who could make a big brand out of Soul Sounds. The rest is history. Now, whenever you four get to the stage, everyone loves your music. I guess, in a way, Lucas helped my mother fulfill her dreams, and it's my priority to help my dad fulfill his."

"It must have been tough with your brother being the center of attention most of the time while you were younger."

Amy shakes her head. "Not so hard, but when I got older it became a problem. Everyone always associated me with him, Lucas Higgins's little sister. I don't want my brand to have that same tag."

"So, Keaton Designs?" I ask, and when she arches a brow, I add, "You told me once. Plus, I saw the tag on Mika's wedding dress the day we worked together."

"Yeah, Keaton Designs," she answers. "It's my grand-dad's name. He always made me feel like I was my own person. He was my favorite person in the whole world and I knew he loved me more than anything. I think it suits my brand well."

"It sure does."

We are soaring over the ocean now, and Amy is the first to look outside. Her mouth gapes and she plasters a hand over it before exclaiming. "Oh my ... Come look at this."

Moving to sit by her side on the chair, I stare outside too. "Waimea Canyon," I say as I admire the look on her face. The steep sides are always magnificent to look at."

"So I've heard ... It's my first time."

She blushes adoringly, only God knows why, and continues staring outside in awe the entire time we are on board, and I watch her also because to me the view of her face is better than that of the Canyon I have seen many times.

Amy slowly turns to face me after a while, and my eyes don't leave hers.

"I don't want to fight being with you anymore, Amy. Can we enjoy the rest of our time here on the island? The outside world will intrude soon enough, but until then, I'd like us to explore this. What do you say?"

She stares me in the eye and breathes, "I'd love that. But I'm scared."

"So am I. But I don't want fear to come between the time we have left here."

After we land, I take us back, holding her hand the whole time, and as I park, I suggest, "We should go to the room," Tension slowly ebbs into my muscles. She nods once, and as we exit the car, she takes my hand and leads the way to the room.

Once inside, leaning closer to her before I can stop myself, I taste her lips. As always, the kiss makes me shiver. I slide a hand to the back of her neck and hold her head steady so I can deepen the kiss.

When we separate, we are both panting, and I groan before kissing her again, then pull her close to the bed, so I can sit while she straddles me. My hands can freely explore her body.

My hunger for her rises as I kiss her lips and move my lips to the side of her neck so I can inhale her scent. She responds to every touch and that makes me want her more.

Her hands move into my hair, she tugs the band holding it into a ponytail away, and combs her fingers through my strands. The feel of her soft touch on my scalp makes me ache with need, so I move my hands under her bottom and press her harder against me so she feels my passion.

10

———

AMY

THE NEXT DAY, WE GO AROUND THE ISLAND'S MAIN market. Dylan buys some spam musubi, and he eats it heartily after sharing some with me. "Hmmm, this is amazing," I compliment after my first bite. "Tastes like sushi."

Strolling the main market hand in hand, we enjoy each other's company and the activity around us for a long time. Dylan looks at ease as he smiles, and we make stops at different local stores to either try out some local dishes or buy items like the lucky charm bracelet I'm now wearing.

His gaze drops to my wrist, and he strokes it for a while before he grins at me, and I grin back. "I've had my fill today, but it won't be complete if I don't try some macadamia nuts. I've always wanted to try those," I say.

At the next stop we make, Dylan buys me some nuts, and we sit on the bench in front of the store and order some beer.

The next few minutes are silent, enjoying our drinks and watching some of the locals walk around the market. Some couples leisurely strolling, people going their own way, trying to get past the crowd. Light music plays inside the store. Resting my chin on my hand, I watch both Dylan tossing nuts and the passersby.

The cool breeze brings great relief to the usually hot sunny afternoons here on the island. Inhaling the clean air, I enjoy the feel of the breeze on my skin. Dylan looks in my direction and smiles at me.

"What's on your mind?" he asks.

"Just wondering what's on yours," I reply. "It's hard to know what's going on in there most times."

"If it isn't about Soul Sounds, then it's about my foundation or about you. It's frankly the first time in a long time, I think about a woman this way. That's not flattery."

"You have a way with words, Dylan," I say with an amused smile. "That works."

Reaching for some nuts at the same time, our hands touch. He lets his thumb stroke my palm before he moves his hand away.

"I don't flatter women, I compliment them," he says to me with a cocky grin. "And I never say what I don't mean."

His words make my insides tingle. Suddenly, a woman comes up behind him, and squeals after taking a good look at his face. "Oh my gosh, you're from Soul Sounds," she says in a high-pitched tone, squealing again before she reaches into her bag for her phone. "Can I get a picture?"

"Sure."

Taking her phone and scooting on his bench, he allows her to sit beside him. Making cute and silly faces, they take selfies together before he returns her phone.

Excited and gushing out, the woman hurries away, and Dylan laughs when he looks in my direction again.

"You must get that a lot."

Over the next few minutes, he tells me about his experiences during his tours, and his approach whenever there are tons of fans waiting to photograph him, or paparazzi wanting to take numerous photos of him when he isn't aware.

Leaving the store, we head for the beach near our hotel. Once again, as Dylan sings in the live band that night, I sit with the crowd and listen to the sound of his voice.

My heart tells me I'm falling for him. There's something gentle about his nature, and nothing is stopping me from letting these feelings grow, but even as I indulge in them, I am still vaguely reminded that it will all come to an end soon.

Dylan has a life of fame, just like my brother, and even though I want recognition too, I don't want it riding on someone else's name. Besides, he is much older than me, so this is a learning experience for me, even though I'm not sure what he is taking from being with me. Soon, our time on the island will be over, then what happens? I have to get to my life in New York and my work, and Dylan has big plans for his band and foundation. *What happens to these memories I'm making now?* It will all end, but I will still cherish the memories. And pray my brother never finds out.

What happens when we leave? Will Dylan even remember our time together? Or is it business as usual for him once it is all over?

As he is singing, he looks at me, and I'm unable to hold back a grin. The melodious twang of his guitar blends with the sound of his voice, and people are laughing and singing along to his song, Heart Strings. The wind around me whips my hair into my face because I'm sitting so close to the flapping waves of the ocean around us and I use both hands to control my strands.

Out of all the noises surrounding me, the loudest is my heart beating rapidly in my chest. Having stopped singing,

Dylan walks over to me again. Pulling me to my feet, he wraps his arms around me, then leads me to the dance floor.

"Hula dancing," he says, reminding me of the night we met at that bar.

Tossing my head back, I laugh and join him in showing my hula moves. The night continues to be the most exciting fun I have ever had.

LATER THAT NIGHT, THE WALK TO MY ROOM IS HAND-IN-hand. As we reach my door, Dylan stops. Taking both my hands, he places them on his chest, moving closer and lifting my chin a bit so he can kiss me tenderly on the lips.

Giving it my all, I kiss him back, and when he pulls away, every nerve in my body hums with desire.

He whispers my name, and I let my hands move down his chest. "Will you come inside?" I ask.

His eyes hold and search mine for a while. I'm about to lower my gaze when he releases a deep groan and nods. Opening my door, we step inside my room. Once the door closes behind us, I'm up in his arms, my legs hugging his waist.

I want to explore his body just as he does mine, I want to feel all he has to offer, and nothing feels better than the pressure building inside me as we find our way to my bed.

As he lays me down, Dylan hikes my legs around his waist again. His hips grind into me when I press into him, and the sweet groan that escapes him makes me want to pleasure him more. With shaky fingers, I take off his T-shirt —which proudly claims, "Keep Calm I'm on a Date"—my breath bursting out of my chest in painful gasps, and I explore his bare skin once his clothes come off.

As I reach for his hardened crotch, his hand grabs mine and places it above my head. I'm at his mercy. Taking off his belt, he wraps it around my wrists. The bind is not too tight, but it's holding, and I shiver in anticipation of what he is to do next.

"Don't move them from there."

His lips follow a trail of kisses down my body, leaving a fiery trail everywhere they touch. Writhing beneath him as he peels my clothes off slowly, I can't help but feel he is torturing me as he takes his time. When he slides a hand between my thighs, I part for him willingly, and his kiss touches the spot where I ache for him.

His fingers probing my already wet folds unleash a deep moan from the depth of my soul.

"Amy," he whispers and brings his lips to my already erect nipples. Kissing me again, more urgently this time, his tongue owns my mouth while I struggle to free myself.

"I want to touch you," I tell him.

His reply is a deep guttural sound that sends shock waves through me. My hips tilt toward his when he frees me, my breasts pressing against his chest and he wraps his hands around my waist, then turns us over so I'm straddling his thighs.

After taking off his shorts, I climb over him again and slowly lower my body to his already ready hardness. Closing his eyes, Dylan releases a deep breath as he fills me. It is easier this time. No pain. I easily adjust to his size and girth. God, who knew something could feel this good? I thought I wouldn't be lucky enough to feel him inside of me again. I'm so glad I was wrong, and I'll enjoy this for as long as I can.

My hands settle on his chest again, his on my hips, holding me steady as a rhythmic dance takes over our bodies. Gliding over him, panting, and sighing, he slides in and out of me. The intense pleasure flowing through me weakens my limbs, making my temperature spike, and toes curl.

Letting out another throaty groan, he turns again and impales me on the bed with his weight. Crying out is all I can do as he kisses the base of my neck, kneads my breasts, and quickens his strokes. Every glide of his body against mine draws me closer to a peaking climax.

I love the rush of blood to the surface of my veins that makes it seem like I'll explode from the heat inside me. His thumb massages my pleasure spot at the apex of my thighs, and I quiver under him.

Leaning down, Dylan enfolds me into his embrace, as I give into the raging pleasure and climax hard around him. His strokes are short and precise now, and I match every one of them.

His kiss is feverish. All my muscles tense as another climax builds inside me.

Sighing as he nibbles on my lower lip, my core contracts against his hardness, and I feel the heat of his seed as he bucks his hips into mine one last time before he collapses to the side of the bed and pulls me along with him.

A languid feeling settles over me, his light caresses make me sigh, I close my eyes and indulge in his scent and heat as he continues to hold me close. The second time was even better than the first and I already thought that had been perfect.

I'm at peace ... It's insane because I've never felt this way, and I'm starting to wonder if this is what love feels like. I remember some lyrics from Soul Sounds song, and I find myself relating to it properly for the first time.

I want to be close to you,

Love me, love me...
Find you in my dreams,
Love me, love me...
Your peace is all I need.... Oohhh...

Dylan starts humming the same song, coincidentally, and it brings a smile to my face.

He lowers his head and looks at me. "Make me yours," he whispers.

I don't know what he means, and I don't care. All the reasons why we shouldn't be together don't apply in this bubble and all I want in that moment is him, so I put my hands on his stomach and let them drift down his body. His eyes close, he inhales sharply, and I feel him bulge a bit in my hands. This man was my first lover. And if it were up to me, he'd be my only. My last.

"You make me yours," I whisper back before I kiss him, slipping my legs around his. My blood turns to liquid desire, with every throbbing cell in my body coming alive again. My thighs part a bit and I push against him so I feel his hot hardness at my center.

"I want you again," he tells me, and I don't need him to say more.

DYLAN

While I'm practicing a new song for the tour, Amy is working in her room. Every minute, my mind wanders to her, and I smile because I always remember our time together. She is so full of life, and passion ... And even though I know all we have to face if we were to stay together, I also know that is a pipe dream. All I want is to explore everything I can think of with her while we are here because her energy is infectious.

This is the best fun I've had in a long time.

Placing a call to our manager, Ken, for the next hour, we go over the details of the tour. He sends me a list of locations after that, and I'll share them with Lucas, Chase, and Jay once we meet up later that evening.

Mika is not at the table with them when I join them at the beach. Chase smiles and hands me a cocktail once a server arrives, and I thank him. As I assess Jay and Chase, the night kings, they don't look too hungover or even overly tired, so the night must have been light.

"Mika?" I ask.

"Off playing with Amy," Jay replies.

Lucas is unusually quiet, so I look in his direction and find him watching me. "Where have you been?" he asks in a light tone.

"Yeah, man, since the wedding, we've seen less of you than of the newlyweds," Jay agrees.

"I've been working on my lyrics and exploring the island," I reply, then drink from my cocktail.

"Have you seen the Hanauma Bay?" Chase asks. "Jay and I visited there yesterday, we got pictures."

Chase passes me his camera, and I look at the pictures he took at the Bay. We continue talking for some time till Amy and Mika join us. As she sits at my side, my attention immediately shifts to her, and I can't deny that it is obvious.

Jay's suspicious look doesn't escape me, but Amy is talking about her plans for the next wedding she will get to design a dress for, and she has my entire attention.

She shows me pictures of Mika in the white backless wedding dress.

"I said it before, and I'll say it again, Mika. You were the most beautiful bride I've ever seen." Mika blushes, causing us all to laugh.

After sharing a group meal, as Amy reaches for a servi-ette to wipe her lips, I move faster and hand it to her. I'm still glancing in her direction every time she speaks, and it's a reflex for me to want to look at her once I hear her voice.

I smile when she makes a silly face, gets on her feet, and does a little dance with her hands because Lucas announces that we should head to a club after our time here.

When she sits back down, laughing, I wipe my thumb over my lip. At this point, I don't care who is watching us, I'm lost in her, and it doesn't bother me.

Our hands brush when we both reach for the wine bottle on the table and I let my hand graze hers before I retreat and let her pick the bottle up. In that moment, all I want is to steal her away from everyone else, take her to my room, and kiss those delectable lips.

Amy's cheeks flush as she relaxes on her chair, and she is quiet for some time before she starts talking with Mika again.

When we get to the club, it's dance time as usual. Lucas teases me about my usual flirting at clubs, but it's not the same tonight. I don't see the need to speak to anyone else, and my eyes are solely on one woman. The only one I want but is not meant for me. The one I plan on enjoying every chance I get for as long as I can... because it will fade. But until then, I'll make the most of it and make sure we both enjoy the ride.

"Never have I ever" comes up and we all play. Amy doesn't drink nearly as much as any of us, but everyone is laughing, obviously getting tipsy. My mind is clearer than day as I watch Amy from my corner of the table.

Nothing beats the warmth in my chest as I watch her, I realize.

After the night fun ends with me driving everyone else back to the hotel, I follow Amy to the back of the building and we sit by the pool.

"I love the night skies," she whispers as she looks up.

Looking at her while she's stargazing, I wonder if the way I'm starting to feel for her will ever change. Words mean little, I learned that early enough. Feelings matter more than anything else and I always focus more on that.

It can't be, I tell myself after a while. Love doesn't exist, it's not real, and the intense need to always be around Amy is simply attraction and fascination. It will fade, right?

My heart fluttering for her is also passion, and the mindless need to make love to her is simply desire.

What else could it be?

She touches my hand and moves close so she can rest her head on my shoulder.

"I love stargazing too," I say, enjoying the moment with her. "And skinny dipping."

Laughing, she stands up so she can slither out of her clothes. I can't hold back my amusement as she lifts me to my feet too and whispers in the sexiest voice I have ever heard, "Come dip with me, then."

Following her into the pool, naked, the cold water does nothing to douse the heat inside of me. Soon, we're kissing deeply, and she is pressed against my body just the way I want her to be.

The next evening, as I'm standing in front of the hotel after Chase, in his signature black jeans and tank top, and Jay, with his usual open Hawaiian shirt and shredded jeans, drive out to spend some time in the main market, I wave at Mika and Lucas when they leave.

Amy has been in her room working the entire day, and I haven't seen her since I left her there this morning. I missed her so I decide to do something about it. Knocking when I reach her room, she immediately opens the door and smiles.

"Hey," she says as she immediately pulls me into the room, and hands me a bowl of office pins. "Here, help me hold this so I can work faster."

Laughing, I take the bowl from her. I can't help teasing her, "I should not have come here if I knew you'd make me work."

"It's only for a minute," Amy replies to me absent-mindedly.

When she looks up again, there's a small frown on her face. Leaning forward, I kiss her forehead. "I'm not complaining."

Smiling, she lowers her eyes to the black full-length dress she is designing. Walking to the table at a corner, she peers down at her sketch pad while I'm standing there holding her pins and waiting.

"Do you think this is lovely?" she asks as she walks back to me and takes the pins away.

"Hmm, I do. I think you're prettier, though," I say, stealing a kiss before she can say anything.

Laughing, she sits on her bed. "I've been working all day. I'm exhausted and hungry."

As I sit beside her, she is swinging her legs. "I think I'll stroll out to get something to eat."

"Why not order in?" I ask, taking her hand.

Every time I'm near Amy, I completely forget every reason I should stay away from her. When we are together, the age difference fades. She is so mature and I feel younger. A boy in his prime.

"I'd like to take a walk," she counters. "Come on, walk with me."

Following her out of the hotel, we walk down the street, no destination in mind. Just being with her is enough to calm me down and I want to enjoy this any time I can. Wanting to avoid recognition, I stand outside as we get to a local supermarket. Amy goes inside and I get distracted by a group of teenagers setting up instruments and mics in front of the store.

As they start singing—one of them is playing the guitar, and the only girl in the group is playing the piano—some passersby drop cash in the bowl in front of them, I smile, approaching just long enough to do the same.

After singing, they do a dance performance. It's refreshing and nice to see young talented people showcase themselves even when they have little.

Soul Sounds started out the same way. My friends and I used to sing at a bar first. Soon, we started getting invites from neighboring bars and restaurants because most of the people who frequented these places enjoyed our music.

When Lucas's mother had chosen to get us a manager, our hobby had changed and turned into something bigger. Looking back now, I realize music used to be a lifeline for me. But now it is life itself.

As the dancers finish their show, and the crowd starts to disperse. I start searching for Amy amongst the crowd. She should be here by now. Not spotting her anywhere, I hurry toward the store to check if she's still in there.

Before I get to the door, a scream comes from the corner of the building. It sounds like a woman in distress, and I start running in that direction. Dashing around the building, I turn to catch a man hovering over someone in a black hoodie. Running in his direction, I kick out my right leg, and push him aside forcefully.

As the woman raises her head, my heart drops as I realize it's Amy. The man curses loudly and starts coming toward us again. Dragging her behind me, my arm juts back and I punch him in the face hard before he can do anything.

Staggering from the blow, he falls on his back, I turn to Amy, ignoring the pain in my knuckles because my mind is frantically racing out of the panic.

"Are you alright? What happened?" My voice is shaking from the adrenaline. The threat is not gone yet, so I can't really focus on her as much as I wish I could. As the man gets on his feet again, I turn sharply, but instead of advancing toward us, he runs in the opposite direction.

"I was watching the dancers, and he came at me, dragged me here, and tried to take money from me," she rasps. Keeping my eyes where that guy disappeared to, I gather her into my arms, running my hands down her body to make sure she is alright for myself.

When I pull back, the bruise on the side of her lip catches my eye and I touch it lightly. "He hurt you," I say. My voice is stiff and my jaw hardens. *That son of a bitch.*

Hugging her again, I feel her shaking her head, trying to deny what is so clear. When my racing heart starts to subside, I finally feel the pain in my hand again. Groaning, I move away from her, trying to flex my fingers, but it hurts too much.

"Are you alright?" she asks as she looks at me. Her eyes widen, her pupils dilate, and the lines of her forehead crease together as the frown on her lips deepens.

It's my time to shake my head. "I think it's broken," I say as I show her my hand. Amy touches it, and I groan again because of the sharp pain. "I can't move my fingers without pain."

"We should get it checked."

I let her lead me around the building and wait till she calls a cab to take us to the nearest clinic we can find. As we arrive, the first person I text is Lucas to let him know where we are.

12
———

AMY

I can't help worrying over Dylan as a doctor examines his fingers. My right hand is on my neck. He flinches when the doctor tries to straighten his hands.

"I'm sorry." I touch his arm. His voice is gruff when he groans from the pain again.

"My guess is your knuckles are broken. If the x-ray confirms it, you'll need a cast and some pain meds," the doctor says.

"No, no cast," Dylan immediately objects. When I touch him again, he faces me and adds. "I have to practice. There's a tour and..." his voice turns into a groan as the doctor is pulling back her hand.

"With that much sensitivity to touch, I'm fairly certain you have a fracture," the woman says. "No cast and you won't heal. You won't be playing anything for a while, sir. I'm sorry."

When she leaves, Dylan groans and shakes his head. His eyes squeeze shut and he rubs his forehead with his left hand. "This is impossible ... I can't afford to not practice now, and a cast will take weeks to heal and .... How do I play?"

"I'm so sorry, Dylan," I whisper as I keep a hand on his shoulder. Tears threaten to run tracks down my face, but I hold them in as best as I can. "This is all my fault. If only I had said yes to eating in. I shouldn't have pushed you to go out. I just..." I'm shaking my head and my body is shaking too.

"It's not your fault," he replies softly, but his voice is tight, and the grimace on his face makes my guilt double. "I'll heal."

Shifting away from me, he lies on the bed. When a nurse returns, they give him some pain meds and move him to another section so they can cast his hand and I sit with him through the procedure till Lucas, Chase, and Jay arrive.

"What happened?" Lucas asks when he gets to us.

Rising to my feet, I start explaining, but Dylan cuts me short. "It's nothing serious, and it'll heal in a few weeks."

"The tour is in less than two weeks," Chase says, voicing everyone's concern.

Lucas shoves his fingers through his hair, and I sigh again. There is a worried look on everyone's face.

"Are you okay?" Lucas's eyes bore into me, reading the guilt on my face maybe. At my weak and lame nod, his gaze doesn't waver.

"I'm fine," I assure him, because this is not about me. With a former nod then mine as he is walking out of the room, Lucas pulls out his phone, and I stay with Dylan, who is unusually quiet now.

When Lucas returns, he says. "I just called Ken, he says he can push back the tour for like two weeks, but that's the best he can do because of the other people involved in hosting us. If when the time comes, your hand still isn't better, then you might not be able to play ... We would need another guitarist to substitute for you while you sing back vocals for me."

Dylan's jaw hardens after Lucas's news, but he doesn't open his eyes or say a thing as he lies on the bed. We stay with him till the doctor returns and checks his cast one last time before clearing him to go.

Later that evening, as I'm sitting with everyone at the beach, my mind is with Dylan, who is not with us.

"I haven't seen him since we got back from the hospital," Jay says.

"He'll be devastated," Mika contributes, not knowing she's only adding to my guilt. "He's been working on perfecting his songs for the tour and now, with his knuckles, he might not get to play."

"What happened anyway?" Lucas asks and faces me. "How did he get hurt because of you?"

"I needed to buy something from the store, so we strolled out, and he defended me from some lunatic trying to steal from me."

"Dylan must have punched him real hard to hurt his knuckles like that," Mika comments.

"Yeah," I reply dryly.

My mind stays with Dylan as we spend some more time at the beach before I return to the hotel to continue working on my designs. Sitting at my table, I stare at my sketchpad for a long time. The designs just don't come to me no matter how hard I try to create one in my head.

After a while, I finally start sketching a prom dress. I focus on creating the curve lines, and I use another colored pencil to map out the sleeves and fancy additions to the side.

Time passes as I sit there and sketch. Later, my eyes

drift to the wall clock. Past nine pm. I'm worried about Dylan, and knowing how much the tour meant to him makes my heart ache for him.

Perhaps I should go to him?

After considering this for a few minutes, I decide to go for it. Changing into another T-shirt and shorts, I head out to his room. When I get to the door, strings of a guitar stream from inside. My heart jumps in my chest because I suspect he is trying to play.

Dylan's head jerks in my direction when I open his door without knocking.

"Dylan," I call as I go to him.

Holding his guitar in one hand, he gives me a stern look when I try to touch him. "What are you doing?" he asks in a stiff voice. His eyes lift to mine, and there's no smile in there. The usual warmth is gone also. "I need to be alone."

"Dylan..."

"Please leave, Amy," he repeats as he turns to his table again and drops his guitar on the floor. Picking up his pen with his left hand, he starts making inscriptions on his notepad, but his hands are shaking, and he can't seem to get it right.

"I could help you write it," I suggest.

"Leave, Amy," he orders, this time in a louder voice. Getting on his feet, he walks to the door and holds it open for me. "Just ... Please let me be."

Exhaling deeply, I walk out of this room even though my heart aches for him.

The door closes behind me. I wait there to hear anything else, but when he groans and curses loudly inside, throwing something that crashes loudly on the ground, I pick up my pace, and run away.

THE NEXT DAY, DYLAN STILL DOESN'T COME OUT OF HIS room, and I need to know he is alright. The other boys are singing as they stroll around the beach, Mika is beside me and she is just as quiet as I am.

"What's on your mind?" she finally asks after a long time. "Are you worried about Dylan?"

Mika is like a psychic most times. It's eerie. When I look at her, there is a knowing smile on her face. "You are, aren't you?"

"Are you not? His tour is only some weeks away, he needs to practice so he can perform, and now he is injured because of me."

We stop and sit by the shore. I stretch out my legs in front of me, and the cool water touches them when it flows in our direction.

"I am, but I've known Dylan for a while now, and he is usually a loner. He doesn't come out much, hardly ever wants to play around, and even when he seems relaxed, music still runs in his mind. He'll be alright, Amy, I'm sure of that. Even if he doesn't play, he'll be alright in the end."

"I tried to help him yesterday, but he was really stiff when he asked me to leave. It's my first time seeing him so grumpy, and I guess it's been on my mind since then."

Mika laughs. "He's usually a grump," she replies. "You care about him a lot, don't you?"

Hesitating only for a second, I nod, and the look Mika gives me spikes my curiosity. "I shouldn't?"

"You should, he's a great guy," she answers.

"But?" I ask when she shrugs, appearing to be holding back.

"Dylan's not a long-term guy," she says. "Are you sure

you want that? And Lucas ... He's definitely going to go crazy once he finds out."

"Because Dylan isn't a long-term guy?"

"Because you're his little sister, and a guy like Dylan is a bit too broody in the real sense of it for you."

Everything Mika says to me only makes me wonder what Dylan's story is like. He has a passion for helping people who have been through domestic violence, and abuse, and most people with such dreams always have a history of abuse themselves.

Is it possible he does?

I don't know much about Dylan, and from what happened when I went to him yesterday, I know now that there's a withdrawn side to him. I had always known, but seeing it in real time was different.

Like a wake-up call. And now it makes me wonder again what will happen when Dylan and I are no longer here in Hawaii. What will happen to our connection? Is it even real for him?

"I can't help it either way," I say to Mika eventually. "I can't get him out of my mind. To me, he's just Dylan, and I think I'm in love with him."

"Love is a beautiful thing," Mika says. "It happens when we least expect it, and if you feel it, that's a good thing."

She smiles, and I feel a bit comforted. Looking at the ocean, I admire the clear blues of the water for some time. Feeling it lap against my skin is indeed comforting, and I wish I could stay here for a long time, peacefully, like this.

Mika joins Lucas and the others when they walk back toward us, but I continue sitting there because I'm enjoying the breeze on my skin and the way it makes me relax.

After some time, the cold seeps into my skin too much,

and I get on my feet, dust my hands over my shorts, and start walking toward the hotel.

Dylan is standing there. His left hand deep in his pocket, and his head raised to the sky. The wind blows against his long hair, he doesn't try to tame the strands that fly all over the place.

How long has he been standing there?

He looks peaceful as I watch him. My heart swells in my chest and starts to beat faster than it should. I take in a deep breath because I need to ease the swelling in my chest.

Slowly, he turns in my direction, and his eyes land on me. Dylan removes his hand from his pocket and turns toward me. As he walks up to me, I'm rooted on the spot.

"Amy..." My name rolls off his lips with a breathlessness that I love.

"Dylan," I call back, meeting his gaze.

He doesn't say anything before he pulls me into his arms and hugs me tight, and I feel like I've come home. "I'm sorry for yesterday," he whispers as he smoothers a hand down the back of my head, then he presses me into him. "I shouldn't have snapped at you like that. I was just really frustrated, and I took it out on you," he explains when he pulls back.

"You did," I reply and frown a little. "I was worried about you, Dylan ... I am still worried about you."

Lifting my hands, I frame them on his cheeks. "I want to help you in any way I can if you'll let me."

His eyes latch onto mine and I'm swept off my feet by their intensity once again.

"There isn't much you can do for me," he says, taking my hand in his and linking our fingers. "Music is my solace, it always has been," he adds as we start walking down the beach again. "Soul Sounds is what music is to me. It's the only way I've been able to escape the torment of what my life was like."

After his statement, he glances my way, and I know he wants to say more, but I wonder if he will.

My heart is pounding in my chest, and every part of me tilts toward him because I really want to know what his past is like.

"Tell me," I whisper. "Tell me all about you, Dylan."

13

———————

DYLAN

Tightening my grip on Amy's hand, I don't want to let go. She is looking at me as we walk down the path. When she asks me to tell her everything, I search for the words because never have I ever gotten to the point where I needed to share myself with any woman before.

Amy is different from anyone else I have ever met. There's something real about the passion in her eyes. The way she laughs when she's with me, how her eyes light up when she smiles. Everything about her seems genuine, and it lures me with a force I cannot deny or control.

"I first started singing to escape a lot of things at home. After school, back then, I used to work at a bar. One day, after a long time of watching your brother and his friends come there to sing for small cash, I decided to substitute for their terrible guitarist who was making them lose a lot of money. That was the start of something amazing for me."

The second I start telling Amy everything, I can't stop. She is quiet the entire time, does not interrupt me, or say a thing as I tell her about my father's job as a pilot, then his resignation after the airline folds, and my mother's obsession with being controlling.

"I was ten when the abuse first started. She would get home so drunk, yell and smash things, then pick on me when my father did not pay any attention to her. At some point, he realized what was happening, so whenever he could, he would take me over to my neighbor's once she got back and brought me back once she was fast asleep on the couch." As I talk, I look at the horizon. There is no way I can talk about something so hurtful, my darkest years, and look at her. The light in my life. A light I know will eventually fade as well.

"I was used to her being hurtful while he was working, but after he stopped working, there were still times when he couldn't save me, and she would insult us both, screaming at him or at me. And, following my father's lead, I would just sit there and take it. She was my mom, so I had to listen, right?" I shrug, attempting to dismiss the hurt the memories still flood me with. Her hand squeezes mine and that simple gesture as a show of support is enough to keep me going.

"Turns out she resented me because she didn't want to have me when she got pregnant, but her parents were conservative, and it was difficult for her to get rid of me. She didn't love me, or my father, but she had to settle, and it was never enough for her.

"After the divorce, and even before, sometimes, when I was lucky enough to have my father home and have it just be the two of us, he tried excusing her behavior while making me see she was wrong about me. About us. But it is hard hearing all those hurtful things for so long and not believe at least some of it, you know?" And I had believed most of them. Some of them I still struggled with, but Lucas and the guys, as well as music, had helped me with most of it.

"Growing up in that house made me see life and love in a light that is not all that bright."

"I'm so sorry, Dylan," Amy finally speaks. "No child should have to go through all of that."

I swallow because my throat is tight just from remembering what it was like when I was younger. "I finally got the courage to leave after I met your brother and the guys. They changed me, gave me more confidence in myself, and that makes me loyal to them more than anything else." I'd do anything for those guys. They and my dad are my families. Forever.

"So, you never saw yourself being anything else? Never had any dreams before music?"

I shake my head. "This is who I am," I say, then start humming our popular song written by Jay, 'This is me'.

Amy laughs and shakes her head. She uses her right hand to move her hair away from her eyes, and I help her, tucking some strands behind her ear and letting my fingers graze her skin for a second before I move her chin and turn her to face me.

"I wrote a new song last night," I tell her. "'Perfect you' is the title."

"I'd love to hear it," she says with a wide grin. "I've been a huge fan of Soul Sounds for a long time, you know? I listen to my brother's demos each time he sends me recordings, and even though I haven't watched any of your live performances yet, I always enjoy what I hear on the radio."

"Secret die-hard fan," I tease, and she laughs hard.

I start singing her some lyrics from my new song, and she's staring deep into my eyes as I do. My voice trails off when I get to the bridge, and I can't sing anymore because the lyrics of that part suddenly make my heart flutter and pound harder than it ever has for her before.

I want you forever, but forever's not long enough if it's real...

In that moment, I don't want to think of anything else but her, so I move, inching my head closer to hers, slowly brushing my lips over hers.

Amy takes control of the kiss then. She slips her tongue into my mouth, and kisses me deeply, slowly pulling away so she can look into my eyes again.

"What you do to me, Amy," I rasp as I pull her close and nuzzle the side of her neck. "You ..."

She stops me with another kiss, and I have nothing else to say. "Let's get to the hotel," she says in a husky tone that makes my pulse jump. My body reacts fiercely to her tone, and I let her link our fingers.

The walk to the hotel is the longest of my life. Our hands brushing builds the passion between us. As we get to her bedroom, she opens the door, letting me in and pushing me against it once we are inside.

Smirking, I admit "I like this," when she slides her hands inside my shirt to touch my abdomen. My muscles grow taut, and I kiss her again, using my good hand to bring her close and press her against me.

Moving away, Amy seductively slips out of her clothes while my eyes move over her body, admiring her curves, the small swell of her breasts, and the tumble of her hair past her slender shoulders.

Walking to the bed and sitting, I pull her toward me so she can sit on my lap. Her breasts are in my face, and I use my tongue on her first while my left hand explores. She starts to spray kisses all over my face. Her hands are in my hair as she moans when my fingers slide over her wet center.

When she rocks her hips against my hands, I groan, murmuring words even I cannot understand as I clamp her waist so she stays steady. Standing up, she pushes me onto the bed and climbs over me.

Taking off my shorts and my shirt, she kisses me till I'm breathless before she lowers her body unto mine.

Closing my eyes, I can't hold a super low moan. Inhaling sharply, I let her set the pace. Our lovemaking is explosive as always, but it's different. She holds my gaze the entire time. She is feisty, and I love it.

Matching her passion, I hold her down so I can stroke her from below, and she moans out loud while her warm core draws me in and makes it impossible for me to hold back my release. Earth-shattering, my climax is unlike anything I have ever felt. It robs me of every logical sense of reasoning, making me cling harder to her, kiss her deeply, and remain buried inside her.

Amy is panting now and quivering on top of me. Her thighs won't stop shaking and I love it. I enjoy the little sounds she makes, and the louder one when I rock into her again, growing hard like I haven't just emptied myself into her.

As she's calming down, I grow hungry for her. Taking her nipple in my mouth, I feast on it. It's impossible to get enough of her taste, her scent. It's like she's done something to me, and my heart no longer belongs to me.

Amy and I lay together after merging our bodies for the second time. I'm still caressing her body and she's breathing deeply now. She's falling asleep, and I don't want to disturb her even though I know my left shoulder will be sore in the morning because her head is resting on my outstretched arm.

Looking at her face, I wish I could touch her slender

nose, but my right hand is in a cast and that alone is frustrating. Deciding to kiss it instead, I drag in a deep breath and fill my insides with her scent.

At some point, I fall asleep too, but it's not a deep one. Her hands touch my face, and I open my eyes. It's too dark for Amy to notice I'm watching her.

Feeling her kisses on the side of my lips, I close my eyes again when she props her head on her hand and stares down at me.

"I'm in love with you, Dylan," she whispers, shocking me to the point where the thudding of my heart in my chest becomes painful.

Keeping my eyes shut, I try to control my breathing, but the pain is too great.

"I love you," she says again.

Don't say that please, I beg. *You can't love me, you can't love a man like me, Amy ....*

"I don't think I'll ever stop," she adds. I sense she is smiling when she sucks in a deep breath, placing her head on my chest again.

Lying still on the bed, I'm too scared to move because she will know I'm awake. My left hand forms a clenched fist, and I start to feel pressure building inside me. She can't love me. She's too young and innocent for me. This was supposed to be something to help me get my fill of her while we are on this island, it was never supposed to go beyond that. Her brother would kill us, for one. And I'm too jaded for her. I know I would eventually hurt her or this feeling would fade sooner or later. And even if I can't understand my own feelings or seem to want her any less, I know better than to think it is love. Love hurts. Love is resentful. Love is constraining. This is not love. Not for me and it can't definitely be love for her. It just can't.

I need to get away.

I must ... I can't breathe, I can't...

The pain in my chest is intense, and I know I will hyperventilate soon. Sweat breaks out on my forehead even though the room is cool. Amy is sighing in her sleep, and although I'm loving the feel of her softness squashing into me, I know I must get away.

I need to.

Slowly, I peel my hand from under her. A soft moan leaves her lips as she flips to her side, and I manage to get out of the bed and dress up without waking her. I make it to the door but stop when she murmurs again. I turn to her, but she's still asleep, so I walk over to the bed, and pull the sheets over her body to cover her properly.

Entering my room, I close the door, and sink to the floor. My left hand moves to my throat, and I rub hard against it. It's like I'm choking on something, and I hate the uncomfortable feeling. It makes me dizzy, and it's overwhelming.

I can't love Amy back. I'm not the kind of man who can risk everything for that single emotion. It did not end well for my father. It's not real.

Shutting my eyes tightly, I try to control my breathing. "It's not real," I chant over and over.

And this is when I know, I must get away from the island. Without re-thinking what I'm about to do, I get on my feet, dashing to the dresser to pick up my phone.

Lucky for me, Ken Daystar is a night crawler, and he's probably still awake when I text him.

I NEED THE NEXT FLIGHT BACK TO SAN JOSE.

. . .

It is the first time in a long while I feel the need to visit my father, and come morning, everyone else will wake up to my text informing them I left the island three days earlier than planned.

Shutting every other thought about to come to mind, I start packing my small bag, followed by a quick shower, getting dressed, and checking my phone to see that Ken sent me details for an early morning flight.

Good thing I'm lucky, I think as I pick my guitar up, hang it, and hurry out to the hotel parking lot where the power bike has been parked for the past two weeks.

I send a text to the rental motorcycle company, giving them the details of my travel so they can come pick it up, then I jump on a cab and ride away without looking back.

14

AMY

THE BUZZING ON MY NIGHTSTAND WAKES ME UP. Groaning, I reach for my phone. "Hey," I say without opening my eyes. When I realize it's Casey on the other end, I sit up on my bed and rub my hand over my eyes.

"Have you seen the news?" she asks.

"Damn it, Casey, where have you been? You ditched me completely and ..."

"I'm sorry, Amy. I know, I know, I'm horrible, I ditched you, but check the entertainment news. When you see it, you'll forget all about what I've done."

"What news?"

"Just check Vogue fashion."

My eyes are wide open now. Ending the call, I go to my browser and do as Casey asked. After scrolling the page for a few seconds, I stumble on a section that reads: Best wedding dress captures of the summer and a picture Mika posted on her social media and the name "Keaton Designs" is listed underneath it.

Gasping, I try to control the ecstatic jump in my pulse. I

go to my social media to check what's trending. Photos of Mika and Lucas's wedding from their page are all over the place. So many comments about her wedding dress, and I can't read them all before my excitement gets the best of me.

"Did you see?" Casey asks as she picks up on the first ring.

"This is huge, Casey. Once we get back to New York, I'll be the one everyone is asking for." After the euphoria runs a bit of its course and we hang up, it really hits me. Keaton Designs finally made it to the top, and no one even knows that I'm Lucas's sister yet.

Joy bursting through me, I dash into my bathroom to brush my teeth, then head out to go give Dylan the good news.

Bursting into his room after a knock, I stop in my tracks. Hotel staff is there, cleaning. "Where's Dylan?" I ask, looking around for clues. Did he change rooms?

The lady shrugs. "I think he checked out this morning. I don't know, but I was asked to clean this room."

Blinking, I try to assimilate what she is telling me. Turning,

I hurry toward Lucas's room. He is coming out as I get there, and Mika is by his side. They are both smiling wide when they see me.

"Did you check your social media?" Mika asks first.

"Your design is trending, and many people are going to your website to compliment your other works," Lucas adds.

"This is great, isn't it?" Mika asks.

They are both smiling as they speak to me, but my mind is someplace else.

"Where's Dylan?" I ask them when I can find my voice

again. Knots form in the pit of my stomach, and I dread the answer Lucas will give me once I see his eyes widen in surprise and his smile fading.

"He left," Lucas said. He glances from Mika to me and adds, "You didn't know he was leaving? You two hung out quite a lot since we got here."

Lucas frowns.

Mika hooks her hand around his and gives him a stern look. She murmurs something, I can't tell what. My hand is shaking.

"You're pale," Mika says to me. I look at her and notice she is worried, but I think it's because Lucas is here, and he doesn't know about Dylan and me.

"I'm fine," I stammer. "I just ... I thought we'd all leave the island together, so I'm shocked that's all."

But I am not really shocked, I'm devastated.

How could he do this? How could he leave like that? Without saying goodbye. How could he do it?

As I'm processing different thoughts at once, my entire world is spinning, but I know I must hold a level of control here. My heart is breaking. Dylan was the first person I thought of sharing the news about my breakthrough with, and he isn't even here.

"Social media is screaming Keaton Designs," I say, pushing Dylan out of my mind and plastering on a great smile. I can only hope that Lucas stops looking at me that way once I smile, which he does. He starts talking about how much attention my brand is going to get now, and how I can handle it all.

Getting a manager, getting more employees, seam-stresses, tailors, the list is endless. I half-listen to it all, but my mind keeps wandering to Dylan no matter how hard I try not to let it.

And I just want to scream.

Last night was magical. I had seen him open his eyes while I was contemplating him, so I had confessed my feelings to him, and it was liberating. Telling him how I felt but waking up without him this morning made me feel like everything we had shared meant nothing.

Did he leave because of that? Is it because I said how I feel? Did he even hear me at all? Was I wrong in my assumption he was awake?

Confusion drowns me. At the same time, ecstasy fills me because of my new success. I wanted to share it with everyone. Dylan, my mom. But now, I can't stop feeling like there's no use.

My day is spent with everyone at the beach, but Dylan is all I think about, and it hurts because I remember him everywhere I turn. I consider calling him, but I cancel that thought. It's obvious he doesn't want me, or he would have, at least, said something to me about leaving.

And leaving without saying goodbye is a strong sign that my worries were right.

After Hawaii, Dylan and I are nothing, and it's going to stay that way. I do not need any more proof than this. I didn't have any promises before, and I am well aware of that. He never asked or offered any more than our time here on the island. I was foolish to think that my feelings growing meant his were doing the same. Now it's time to grow up and let go of the dream. As if it were that easy...

We leave the island three days after Dylan, and I have still not heard from him. Lucas and Jay are talking about the details of the tour as we fly in Soul Sounds private jet. The first drop-off is in New York so I can get back to work, and then Jay and Chase will return to San Jose before Mika and Lucas fly to Greece for their honeymoon.

Work will be busy these coming weeks, and I hope it's enough to keep me from thinking about Dylan and missing him like crazy. Sometimes, I catch myself glancing at my phone, expecting a call or text.

He could easily get my contact from anyone here if he really wanted to talk to me. But each passing hour is proof enough he is not interested.

Closing my eyes, I will my mind to stop spinning. I want to sleep. Make sure the nine hours I'll spend on the jet run quickly, but it proves hard. And when sleep finally comes, Dylan fills my dreams. His eyes are piercing mine, and his soft voice, as he makes love to me, is soothing. He is a man with so much passion, and I fell for that from the start —for his charming voice and passionate eyes.

His touch.

Deep sleep is not happening, so I just give up.

Mika comes into the cabin and sits beside me on the bed. "You're in love with him, and he left without a word," she says to me. "I understand how that feels, Amy."

Placing a hand on my shoulder, her eyes are sincere as she smiles at me. "It'll get better with time. The pain will fade, and you will cherish the memories you have with him."

"Why did he have to run?" I ask. "I just don't understand it. Last night was ..."

I stop myself before I can say more, then sigh and close my eyes. "I'll be fine ... I'm fine," I murmur.

"You will be," Mika encourages. "And you've got a lot on your plate now. You'll get into new heights with your fashion, and you'll make the brand for yourself just like you've always wanted. Everything else will get better."

I sincerely doubt it will. It doesn't seem like I will forget Dylan soon, but if this is what he wants, then I have to adjust.

By the time I arrive in New York and get to my apartment, there are a lot of emails waiting for my attention, including three from top fashion brands wanting to collaborate and one from a top celebrity manager wanting me to design for his client.

Sighing, I stare at the emails for a second, drag in a deep breath, and dive right into replying without even taking a moment to unpack my bags and rest from the jet lag.

After a fitful night, Casey drops by, and she brings me a cake to apologize for ditching me in Hawaii.

"My two weeks there were full of adventure, but you won't believe what happened to me there." She shows me the ring on her finger. "I got married," she adds with a squeal. "I'm freaking out, but I don't know what to do, and I also think I'm excited."

Casey runs a fashion blog. We first met in freshman year and have been friends ever since. We are both rounding up our final year, and Casey is my biggest supporter.

"You met a guy and got married in Hawaii?" I ask, letting her into the house.

"And now I'm supposed to be getting divorced, but I can't. It was one drunken night, we had fun, and now he doesn't want to get a divorce," she says and makes a dramatic wave of her hand. "What's worse is that he's Leonardo Richie."

I laugh, at first, because she sounds ridiculous. Leonardo Richie is a legend. Richie Couture is the holy grail of modern-day historic fashion. He is not just a legend, he is an icon and a star, and a very popular designer in the entire industry.

"You're kidding," I say to Casey and fold my hands over my chest. My problems, suddenly, don't seem so great anymore.

"I'm not," she replies, then shows me the diamond on her finger again. "He had this with him that night, and we got married then and there."

I laugh again, this time, I shake my head, combing my fingers through my hair. "You realize you sound crazy right now?" I ask my friend.

Reaching into her bag, Casey takes out a polaroid. "Here, this is proof enough," she says and hands it over to me.

Leonardo's smile stares back at me. Those steely blue eyes are remarkable, and so is the flash of dimple on his left cheek, and that popular smile.

"Holy shit, it's him," I gasp.

"I'm not kidding."

She sighs. "I don't know what to do," she says as she walks into my living room. Sitting down, she looks around my table and asks, "Working?"

"Turns out I'm now sought after," I say with a smile.

Casey's proud look makes me laugh. She brings out a bottle from her bag. "Oops, before I forget, we should celebrate," she says, sashaying into my kitchen to get two wine glasses. "To Keaton Designs," she says as she pours us both wine, lifting her glass so we can clink.

Dad and Granddad, this is for you, I think.

"To Keaton Designs," I reply, then sip from my glass. The rest of the day with Casey is fun. She is always bubbly, and I enjoy her company. As for my pain, if I don't talk about it, it will go away.

Later, after Casey falls asleep in my room, I'm left staring at my ceiling, thinking once again about Dylan and the warmth he made me feel.

15

DYLAN

Staying a few days with my dad reminds me of how amazing he always is. I'm sitting in his guest room, staring outside the window with my guitar in one hand, when he brings me a cup of coffee.

"Thanks, Dad," I say and take the cup from him. After sipping, I set it on the table and my gaze drops to the cast on my hand.

"Can I sign that?" he asks in a light tone. Laughing, I extend my hand for him to sign. He picks a marker up and scribbles his signature and name on it.

When he smiles at me again, he adds, "Must be hard for you, since you can't play for now."

"It's been a week," I say. "I still have to leave it on for another two, then go for another check to make sure it's fine."

"It will be fine," he tells me, then sits on the bed. "And you'll go for your tour and be excellent like you always are."

Smiling at him again, I give him a soft nod. For a few seconds, we don't say anything to each other, but my mind wanders, and I find myself thinking of Amy again.

She is always on my mind, and whenever I think of her, I remember everything we shared, our time together, her smile, her scent, the feel of her, her gentle tone when she said she loved me.

Replaying her confession in my head makes me shiver slightly, and I hate the tingle that enters my heart just from remembering hearing those words.

"Do you ever regret falling in love with Mom?" I suddenly ask.

Arching a brow, my dad looks at me for a while, then takes off his glasses. "You've never asked me about your mother before. Not even once in the last fifteen years since the divorce," he says.

"I've never been curious, never wanted to know, but I want to now," I reply to him.

Dropping my guitar, I face him completely, as he rubs his forehead. "If it's true love, then you never regret it," he replies.

"What does that mean?" His reply confuses me more, and I don't know what to make of it. "Do you regret loving her, then?"

Shaking his head, his eyes soften. "I still love your mother. I fell in love with her because she was young and free. She used to want so much out of life, dreamed of being a model ... Walking the biggest runway shows and attending the best red-carpet events. Turns out, my love changed her. She was too young for the kind of love and passion I had for her, and after she had you, she felt restrained. She hated that, and she hated me for it.

"It's so easy for those strong emotions to turn to something else. And when you feel them, most times, you have no control. I loved your mother ... I still love her, but I can't say it's the same passionate love with everything that happened. So much time has passed now. What I can say is that I don't regret loving her. Never have."

"Not even once?" I ask.

"Not even once."

My mind keeps conjuring Amy and how it felt to be around her. Would I ever grow to regret her if I had stayed? If things had turned out differently?

I'm pulled out of my thoughts when he asks, "Do you love someone? Is that what this is about?"

I consider telling him about Amy for a second but decide against it because talking about her will only make it more difficult to forget her. It is already hard as it is, I don't want to make it impossible.

"No, that's not it," I lie. "I just wonder why. After everything that happened, you still keep that picture of all of us together on your nightstand."

"I love that picture, Dylan. You were three then, and you were the happiest part of my life ... You still are, Son."

My father smiles at me and puts a hand on my shoulder. "Soon, you'll meet someone amazing, and you'll love her and spend the rest of your life loving her, Son," he says. "I can't wait till you find that. You deserve such happiness, and a life full of love and excitement..."

I don't want to diminish his joy by telling him that his dreams will never come true. I have no intentions of loving a woman and risk getting hurt or abused as my father did.

What's the point?

The feeling will fade eventually, either for me or for the woman, and things will get messy and scary, and every warmth and joy we feel at the start will fade and there will be nothing left.

I rather remember Amy as I do right now ... Loving, soft,

and happy. At night, I dream of her smile, and her passionate response when I made love to her. There are flashes of her in my memory whenever I'm not conscious of it, and even when I write lyrics, I'm thinking of her.

I don't want to think of her and have any regrets, and I fear that's what would happen if things got deeper than they already were.

I love you; I remember her voice and it leaves an ache in my heart. There's nothing I can do to take it away, so I must get used to it.

Long after my dad leaves, I stay in the room and perfect the lyrics of my new song. Next week, the studio sessions will start, and we have less than a month before the tour that is supposed to last three months.

Once I dive into work, I am sure I will forget all about her. *I hope I will* because right now, she is the one constant thought on my mind and it's tormenting.

Two weeks later, I go to a hospital to get my cast removed. The doctor's pleased look as he stares at the x-ray makes me hopeful.

"Your fingers look great, but you'll still have to take it easy on the strings to avoid pain."

"Can I play or not?" I ask the doctor. My father is sitting with me, and he puts a hand over mine when I ask. Looking at him, I don't bother hiding the fearful expression on my face. "I need to be able to play," I say.

"You can play, but you need to tone it down a bit for a couple of weeks. Also, you might be missing some dexterity, I can't be certain until you try to play and see for yourself."

I press my lips together, then flex my wrists and fingers. "Everything seems fine," I say.

"Then I'll write you a prescription for pain medication, in case anything comes up."

After the visit to the hospital, I drive down to the studio with my dad. Jay and Chase are already here, horsing around and flirting with all the ladies, as always. Lucas isn't here because he's not back from Greece yet, but we can start the practice without him till it's time for the demo.

When time comes, dragging in a deep breath, I put my fingers on the strings. Chase starts with the drums, and Jay follows with the bass before I start singing. The melodious sound of the instruments blending gets me in the mood, and I'm tapping my foot on the floor now, getting ready to play with the strings of my guitar.

As my cue comes, the flow is disrupted as I miss the note. I get frustrated, but we start all over again and I warm myself up, only to get it wrong again. Except this time, my fingers hurt.

Groaning, I stop playing, then stare at my fingers for a while. Everyone is looking at me now with concern, and a bare-chested Jay steps forward. Always shirtless or with his Hawaiians hanging open, he loves showing off his abs to whoever is willing to drool over them. "Does it hurt?" he asks.

"I think I just need to warm up to it," I reply. "My fingers feel a bit stiff."

I give Jay and Chase a shaky smile. Outside, Ken and my father are watching intently too, and I smile at them before attempting to play again.

Flopping a third time, I groan and curse under my breath.

Chase comes to my side. He tries to touch my shoulder, but I snap at him, "Just … Get away from me." Grunting, I continue flexing my fingers to ease them up.

My stomach hardens, and pain radiates from the way I clench my jaw. "I'll get it right," I say adamantly, and we start the song again.

I'm finally getting it right until I miss another string and groan louder because it feels like my fingers are about to snap in two.

"Dylan…" Chase calls. "Maybe we should try tomorrow, or…"

"I'm fine," I snap at him. "Jesus!" I drop the guitar.

"Maybe you need a break," Jay adds, supporting Chase, of course. Those two seem to share a mind.

I shake my head. My growing irritation making me glare at them. "I'll get it right," I say and I'm about to try again when Chase moves, taking the guitar from me.

"What do you think you're doing?" I say at the top of my voice.

Before the situation escalates any further, Ken enters the recording room and steps between me and Chase.

"Step aside, Dylan," he says, and I retreat without another word, turning and storming out of the studio. Getting to my car, I enter, close the door, and lower my head to the steering wheel.

What the hell is wrong with me?

Lifting my head again, I stare at my fingers, and I focus on them for a long time. I am frustrated, I'm mad at myself, but most of all, I'm scared. What if I can't play anymore?

A few knocks on the passenger seat window pull me from my head. My dad is standing outside, so I unlock the door for him.

He enters, closing the door, and stays quiet for a while before I look at him.

"I need to be able to play, Dad," I say in a low voice.

"I know," he replies. "Keep practicing it, and you'll get back in your game," he says. "Let's get you back home first, and you take those pain meds you were given. Then you try again. I asked Ken for the day off, so they'll practice without you."

We drive down to my penthouse on Santana Row, and once inside, I head to my bedroom while my dad stays in the living room.

I spend the rest of my day lying in bed. Each time I close my eyes, I remember playing the guitar on the beach and the smile on Amy's lips as she watched me.

Time is rolling by slowly, but I can still remember every detail of her face, her body, and her scent. *It's a part of me now*. I am also getting used to seeing her in my dreams.

A lonely ache spreads through my heart. Ignoring it, I flip over to my side on the bed, and close my eyes. Amy invades my thoughts immediately and with no hope of getting her out of my mind, I pick up my phone and scroll to her social media.

Keaton Designs is trending on almost every social media outlet now, and recently, I overheard Chase and Jay talking about a promotional video clip of Amy on some fashion blog.

She's growing in her field, and I am excited for her. Amy's designs show so much potential, and Mika's wedding dress served as the perfect break-out for her. I know she is only just beginning. And for a second I wonder what it would be like to be there beside her to enjoy this win with her. But I soon shut it off.

Later that evening, I try to play again. This time, go half

the song without feeling any stiffness or missing any notes, so I decide to dedicate my entire time to practice.

At least this way, I won't think about Amy so much.

I was wrong. The slightest idle moment I get, and she pops up in my mind. Soon, I find myself writing a solo song about her and how she makes me feel.

16

___

AMY

"I NEED THE ENTIRE SHOW TO BE PERFECT," I TELL Casey as we stand backstage in the auditorium venue for my first fashion show.

"I know how much this means to you, Amy, trust me, I won't let you down," Casey says with a smile. When the frown on my face doesn't lower, she nudges me on the shoulder. "I mean it. I won't let you down."

I manage a laugh and sigh as Casey walks away. This is a dream come true for me. I am collaborating with a renowned fashion brand for this runway show, and even though most of the designs are for them, it is still a great chance for me because a lot of top models will wear my designs, and many prominent celebrities might like them just from the exhibit.

I am nervous, I can't deny it, and the rumbling in the pit of my stomach will not stop. It has been this way for a few days now, and I don't know what's wrong.

Looking around again, I try to make sure everything is set. The lighting group is backstage, the models are in the dressing room, and the main designer is not yet here, but as soon as she arrives, the show will begin.

I have worked my ass off for this, I think to myself, dragging in a deep breath. It will go perfectly. Going back to the dressing room, I check on the models. They are twenty-seven in number, each of them ready for the night, I smile as one of the stylists looks at me. Jean had the cutest smile I have ever seen, and a French accent that makes him difficult to understand sometimes, but since we've been working together for over a month now, planning the show, I'm starting to get used to the way he speaks.

"Nervous, ma chère?" Jean asks me. "You look pale when you should be flushed," he continues. "Come on now, I'll add some color to those cheeks of yours."

He pulls me to a chair before I can protest, then he adds powder and some concealer to my face. My stomach rumbles again, and I mutter, "Oh boy," before closing my eyes.

There's bile high up in my throat, and it feels like I need to puke before I can feel relieved. I'm also feeling faint beside the paleness and even though I think I'm simply tired and weak from the stress of the past two weeks, I know deep down it might be more.

I can't afford to be sick right now.

"You don't look so good, ma petite chou, maybe you need some fresh air?" Jean suggests.

I nod and rise to my feet again. "Yeah, I think I do."

My head wobbles when I stand, and I swoon.

"Woah," Jean exclaims, holding me steady. "Careful, bijou."

As I hold, he drops his hand from my arm. "I need some air."

Walk out of the dressing room, hand on my temple, I

hurry to the back exit of the building. Once outside, dropping my hands on my knees, I exhale a deep breath.

This past month has been hectic, working long hours every day on numerous design and style inspirations with little rest, and in the few hours I allowed myself to sleep, I thought and dreamed of Dylan. It was hard turning on the TV and seeing his past shows come on or listening to his songs on the radio. It's like the Universe is rubbing it in. And e

ach time that happens, I remember our time together, our passion, and how my heart beat faster whenever he was close to me.

And how all of that meant nothing to him.

It is hard to accept that he thought little of what we shared, but I knew I could get used to it in the end. I may be younger and I may be more inexperienced, but I'm resilient, and if I can get through this, I can get through anything, so I just have to keep pushing through.

Straightening again and sucking in another deep breath to regain control of my shaky insides, I walk back into the building to continue with the preparations.

The main show kicks off at seven pm, and I want everything in place before my partners arrive. Casey is busy with the backstage sounds, and lighting setup team, and I am with the models, handing their stylist the dresses for the walk.

My neck muscles ache, but I ignore it, blaming it on my tension and stress. The need to make sure all of this is perfect is all I can think of.

My mom will be here soon, and I am expecting a call from Mika and Lucas who promised to call me before the start of the evening. Thinking of Lucas brings Dylan to my mind, as if I need any more reminders. I wonder how he is doing and if he is playing. *Is his hand alright?*

It has to be.

My phone rings a few minutes to seven pm. Stepping away from Lisa, the brand's lead designer working with me, I take the call. It's Mika and Lucas, and their brilliant smiles light up my screen as I wave at them.

"Hey star girl," Mika calls in a singing voice. "I'm cheering for you, and set to watch your exhibition," she said.

"This is amazing, Amy, soon you'll be on the Paris Fashion Show or one of those things you girls chat about.

"Fashion week," Mika corrects, and we all laugh at Lucas's silly expression for a second.

"I don't have much time, guys, but it means a lot to me that you called," I say, adjusting the earpiece I'm wearing.

"Is mom there?"

"Not yet, but I got a call and she's going to be here soon. I sent a pickup to get her from the airport."

"Amazing," Mika comments.

Ending the call after chatting with them for a while longer, I head inside to continue working. The show starts at the set time, and I'm watching from backstage as each model walks the runway with my designs first before the main brand designs.

Casey is beside me wearing the same excited expression. Frame my mouth with my hands, I hold my breath to see the crowd's reaction when my last design comes on stage. When they all erupt into loud applause, I feel a rush of adrenaline.

This is a dream come true.

I can't control my excitement as the thunderous sounds of their applause blends in with the music playing in the background. The music continues while I slowly walk toward the stage with Lisa.

Taking my hand, she guides me as we sashay together to the front, where I bow my head a bit while Lisa does a dramatic bow. The smiles on everyone's faces are enough to have my pulse pounding. My skin feels like it's boiling all of a sudden but it must be all the excitement and rush of fulfillment clouding every other feeling coursing through me.

My eyes scan the crowd as I smile, and I spot my mother cheering with joy too. Her wide smile, and the excitement on her face fill me with joy. It's the first time I've seen her this focused on me.

I did it ... I brought life to the designs.

Remembering my father and grandfather in this moment, I wish they were standing there in the crowd with my mother. Together, they would cheer for me, and later tonight, they would tell me how proud they were. My vision blurs while I'm smiling, and I suddenly feel light-headed.

The last thing I remember as I drop to the ground is the silent hush that overcomes the entire auditorium, then a scream from someone that sounds like my mother.

THE NEXT TIME I AM CONSCIOUS, MY MOTHER IS holding my right hand, and Casey is holding the other. Groaning, I slowly try to sit up, but Casey's hands hold me back down.

"You're not allowed to sit up," my mother says as she moves closer to my side. "Jesus, Amy, you scared the crap out of everyone."

"The show?" My head is pounding, but I have to know. "Where's Lisa?"

"Is that what you're worried about right now?" my mother scolds. "You've been sick, and you kept quiet about it?"

The door opens and interrupts her from nagging some more. Sighing in relief, I close my eyes again, wishing I could go back to the solace of my unconsciousness. My head is about to split in two now, and my throat is parched.

Lifting a hand to my forehead, my temperature is not so high anymore. "What happened?" I ask in a soft voice as the doctor gets to our side.

"Good news is that you're not dying," the doctor says to me with a smile. "Congratulations are in order, though. You're having a baby."

I freeze at first, then my eyes snap open wider to see Casey's jaw drop and my mother's eyes widen.

"What?" they croak at the same time before I burst into a loud round of laughter that makes my sides hurt. My laugh ends with a cough, and I put a hand on my chest to pat it a bit.

"What are you talking about, doctor? That's impossible, I'm on the pill."

"Well, pill or not, blood tests don't lie. You're pregnant. I'm sure you understand the pill is not a hundred percent accurate," she replies, still maintaining her smile. "But to make sure everything is okay with the baby, I'm requesting an ultrasound, of course. That way, you can see things for yourself too."

Casey covers her mouth with both hands, and my mother shrinks further into her seat. My hand moves to my stomach, and I touch it before saying. "I'm pregnant?"

"I think we've already established that," Casey exclaims.

"This is insane," she adds, then looks from me to my mom. "Were you trying? I didn't even know you were seeing someone."

"Can I be alone with the doctor, please?" I ask Casey, then turn to my mom. "I ... I need to be alone please."

My mother is still quiet, but sighing, she gets on her feet, and leads Casey out of the room. Alone with the doctor now, I ask. "How far along am I?"

"The ultrasound will tell. Or if you know when you last had your period, that would help too. Miss, you have to understand that if this isn't planned, you have options..."

"Are you kidding me?" I interrupt her as my smile widens. "I'm pregnant. I mean, it's a shock, yes, and it feels like my entire world is spinning right now, but then again, there's this rush ... It feels like I'm on cloud nine, and the way I've been feeling these past few weeks is starting to make sense. Also, I'm thinking, and I'm ... I don't know what to do, but I'm excited, and I don't know if I should feel that but it's all coming to me at once, and...."

My meltdown ends in sobs, and as I burst into a long one, the door opens again, and my mother comes into the room.

"I said I want to be alone, Mom," I cry louder, but she ignores me, coming to my side, and putting her arms around me.

"It's alright, Amy," she whispers. "It's alright to feel shocked and confused. It's alright to feel scared and excited all at once.... It's normal."

I can't stop sobbing into her shoulders for a long time. The doctor leaves us, and Casey comes back into the room at some point to hold my hand.

As my tears finally subside, sniffing, I wipe my face with

both hands. "I don't want to tell anyone about this yet, Mom," I say to her. "Let's keep this between us three."

My mother nods, and so does Casey. "I mean it. Not even Lucas. No one." She looks me in the eye, trying to understand, but nods when I say nothing else.

They are still standing beside me when, sucking in a deep breath, I add, "Let's do the ultrasound."

Finding out about the baby is a shock at first but as the first images come up on the monitor, I gasp, and my heart melts instantly. "She's so little," I whisper in a tiny voice.

The doctor informs me of the changes my body will experience before prescribing my prenatal vitamins and some supplements for my weakness, telling me to rest.

Casey is in charge of handling the work details after the fashion show while I take the week off to rest. My mother stays in New York with me, and we use the time as a chance for our relationship to start to blossom again.

Whenever I'm alone, my mind wanders to my baby and then to Dylan.

How would he react if he ever found out about the baby?

I remember how he told me his story and him telling me he wasn't looking for anyone and didn't want children. Dylan couldn't accept my love. That night when I whispered those words to him, I'm almost sure he was awake, and I had hoped he would respond, but he didn't.

I can't tell him about the baby, I know that. Not only did he make it clear it is not something he wants, but he's also too focused on his tour and his foundation. Besides, if he wanted to know how I was, he would have reached out to me by now. It hurt for so long to know he didn't want me. Still does. But on the bright side, now I have something to hold unto from our time together. My baby is the best part of the memories we made, and I plan to cherish it forever.

Sometimes, when I'm weaker, I consider reaching out to Dylan. About six weeks have passed, and I miss him terribly. But I stay strong and I never do.

Joining me in the living room where I am seated sometime later, my mom hands me a glass of freshly made juice before sitting on the couch next to me.

"How are you feeling?" she asks.

I shrug. "Conflicted," I respond. "I wish I could tell the father, but he ... He didn't want me, Mom, and there's nothing I can do to change that. He also mentioned to me once he didn't want to have kids."

Her hand covers mine. "You're a strong woman, Amy. I've watched you grow, and fight to pave your own way regardless of me or anyone else. You can do this alone if it's what you want, and you should know you have my support always, no matter what."

Staring into her eyes, I whisper, "Thanks, Mom." Her words warm my heart. "I love you."

"I love you too, honey."

This week is the first time in my life that I feel like my mom cares about me as a person. As her arms come around me, I sigh, snuggling into her embrace. Comforting words are what I need to heal my heart right now.

17

———

DYLAN

THE SHOW ENDS WITH ME PERFORMING TO THE CROWD. Hearing them sing along with me is enough to light up my evening and make my heart swell with joy. The adrenaline coursing through me is as if I am standing on a high cliff, and the wind blowing against me is the rush that I feel in my veins.

My fans singing alongside me is the best sound in the world. Chase and Jay are playing with me and Lucas has performed his part and left when the second call-back was about to start because he had a family emergency or something to deal with over the phone. My focus is on playing the guitar and singing at the same time, not wanting to think about if this is something regarding Mika or other family members.

Since the cast came off, I have practiced hard making it easier and easier to switch from singing to simply playing the guitar. As the last song ends on our second call-back, the fans are still raging and screaming their love for Soul Sounds as our bodyguards guide us out of the area to our waiting limo.

Once inside, my eyes close with a sigh. I zone out from my surroundings as Jay and Chase are talking about their time on stage, and how much they are excited about the next performance in three days.

My mind drifts to Amy. Now I wonder if Lucas's emergency wasn't about her.

The second she enters my mind; I can't get her out. The encouraging smile on her face when she watched me sing at the beach, front and center. She is my muse now, and I think of her all the time.

My phone starts ringing. Taking it out of my pocket, I take the call.

"Dylan." Her soft voice on the other side makes my heart lurch painfully in my chest. Ringing in my ears for a second, it sends a shiver down my spine. I can't speak because I'm scared that I'll beg her to take me back if I say anything.

"Dylan, are you there?"

Swallowing hard, I close my eyes. "Yes ... Yes, I am."

She falls silent again, and when her voice comes, it croaks, even though I hear her clearly. "I miss you," she says. "Dylan, I miss you."

"I'm sorry," I respond. Sniffing hard, I rub a hand over my chin.

I end the call before she can say anything else.

Clearing my throat, I say, "Stop the car," interrupting the joke Jay is telling. Jay is always the fun one. He had suggested a night out for fun earlier and our driver was heading there. Except, I no longer feel like hanging out.

Chase tries to reason, "Where are you going? It's night, and we're in Denver. You can't just leave the rest of us and go someplace else."

"I need some air," I reply, ignoring Chase's reasonable thinking.

"Come on, man. You can't seriously want us to just let you out in the middle of an unknown city. That's nuts!"

"Yeah, D-man. Come with us. It will be epic," Jay adds.

As the driver pulls up to the curb, they give up and let me out of the limo. As the limo drives away, I start walking back in the direction we drove past. I'm wearing a hoodie over the tank top I used while performing earlier. Pulling the cap over my head, I stuff my hands into the pocket.

Taking out my phone after walking for a long time, I search for the nearest beach with fewer activities. Finding one, I order an uber and go there.

The windy night is just the right kind of atmosphere I need. Inhaling deeply, I fill my lungs with its crispness, then raise my head to the sky and exhale deeply.

Amy, I think. *I miss you too. So much.* Saying these words to her won't change a thing. I can't be the man Amy wants. A man with hopes and joy. A man who can commit to a life with her. One full of laughter and kids. She deserves someone better. Lighter. Someone closer to her age, less jaded.

I don't believe it will last. I know it won't, and I can't risk getting hurt or hurting her.

She has to find someone who can take the chance, and it would be selfish of me to make her think there is a chance between us, so I must stay away.

I just wish I could convince myself of this.

Watching her ongoing success makes me happy and proud because she's doing so well, but deep down, I'm not happy because I want to share those moments with her. I want to laugh when she does, and I want her to smile at me, flush when I touch her. Memories of our time together never leave me, and there is nothing I can do about it.

My phone rings after a long time of standing at the beach alone, and I take the call from our manager, Ken Daystar.

"Where are you?" he asks.

"Do you need me for something?" I ask instead.

"Show up for an interview with Sawyer Fischer by eleven am tomorrow. A pick-up will be in front of your hotel. They need you there with your guitar to charm the hearts of our fans worldwide."

"Do I have to do it?" I ask, rubbing the back of my neck. "I don't feel like talking about myself to anyone."

"This is the best chance your foundation's got for a break-out. You can let the whole world know your plans, man. Come on, haven't you heard of Sawyer Fischer?"

"No," I reply in a muffled tone.

"Google him, and show up," Ken answers, then ends the call. So, I

do and turns out he's one of the most watched inter-viewers currently, and I was lucky to get on his show.

Claps from the audience warm me after I play them a hit song from our second album titled 'Love yours'. Smiling at me, Sawyer Fischer claps too.

"That was amazing, Dylan. No wonder you have the hearts of the entire country," he says. Laughing at his comment, I comb my fingers through my hair before he looks at my T-shirt and adds. "Your shirt says, 'It's too late to not fall for me'. I think that's true ... Really true, considering you also have many exquisite ladies around you all the time."

Smiling, I let the question hang. I know he is trying to bring up my love life. Jay and Chase are watching from the crowd in the front row, and Lucas prefers to watch the show with Mika. I'm feeling a bit overwhelmed because this is a dream come true for me.

Having a platform to tell the world my intentions and plans for families like the one I grew up in is important, and I'm about to make that dream come true.

"So, tell me, Dylan, is it every woman who falls for you like your shirt says that wins your heart too? Or have you found that special someone that can make you give up anything?"

I wave my hand. "No special someone," I answer with a grin. "Not yet."

The crowd's response to that is a mix of male groans and female cheers and it makes me laugh. "Hopefully, someday," I say, not wanting to give any more than that.

"How about the rumors of a blooming romance some-where in the islands of Hawaii?" Sawyer asks.

His question shocks me, but I keep my smile and shake my head. "There's a lot of those, though," I answer. "Blooming romances and flings."

"So, you don't deny them?"

"I don't."

The interview is a bit light-hearted till the end when Sawyer asks me about my motivation and dreams as America's Star Guitarist.

"It's always been my dream, and that of my soul brothers, to help people. Soul Sounds is a platform for me. If I can reach that broken heart, or that mending soul through my lyrics or sounds, then I'm happy. But most importantly, is the foundation I'm starting ... A platform for families, kids, and women, all over the world who need to share their experiences and stories of broken relationships. I want to inspire them all and share with them the same sounds that helped heal my heart."

The silence in the room shows how much this revelation matters, Sawyer has a solemn expression when he asks, "Are you saying you had a rough past?"

Swallowing hard, I exhale before linking my fingers and giving him the answer to his question. "I did, and trust me, it's never pretty for any child or person to experience that."

Not needing to go into details at that point because the interview is about to wrap up, I hand out the website to my foundation, knowing it will be displayed on the screen for viewers all over the world to see and have access to.

Jay and Chase join me on the stage at the end of the two-hour interview and together, we perform a song for them before leaving the stage.

As we're leaving, Jay's arm comes around my shoulder briefly, as he jokes. "You're a philanthropist now, man."

"We all are," I reply, then we laugh. Even though It's been difficult keeping up with the fun since the start of the tour, it's the first time I genuinely feel a bit relieved, so I suggest in the spur of the moment. "Let's party...."

The bar that evening is Ken's suggestion. There's lots of booze, music, and women, but unlike so many times before, there's no one to catch my attention.

Having drunk way too much, I was still not able to drown my memories. Staggering toward our limo later, Jay and Chase hold me steady.

"Dude, you never drink. What the hell happened to you?" Jay's voice sounds amused.

"Amy," I whisper. "It's all Amy's fault." I'm not fully

conscious of what I'm saying, but saying her name makes me smile. "Amy ... I miss you. Where are you?"

As I get into the limo, her image is all I see. It's like she's taken over and the world no longer exists. "My Amy, so pretty."

"D-man, you are really and truly wasted," Jay teases.

"Whoever this Amy is, it's a good thing she can't see you now." Chase claims, and I have the sudden urge to see her. But she is so far away...

"I know. I'm going to call her."

"Bad idea, man." I frown at Chase. Why doesn't he want me to call Amy?

"It's the middle of the night. She'll be asleep."

Oh, right. Nodding, I state firmly, "I'll text her then." And I start looking for my phone.

As I wake up, two questions pop immediately into my head.

One – What are my friends doing in my room? Creepers.

Two – Why are they staring at me with wide, gawking eyes?

Sitting up in bed, dread fills me to the core.

"Shit, did I do something stupid last night?" I ask, rubbing my forehead and stroking my hair. "Tell me I didn't do something crazy." My head is banging from the hangover, and the expression on my friends' faces makes me shudder.

"You kept calling Amy, the entire night, Dylan," Jay answers first. "You kept asking for Amy, and you even drunk texted her. We tried to stop you, but..."

He brings my phone to me and shows me the text as he adds. "We couldn't. You decked Chase when he tried to snatch your phone."

Chase points at his eye, and I groan when I see the black blotch under his eyelids.

"Ouch," I comment. "I'm so sorry, man."

"It's fine," Chase answers. "It's just ... We didn't know you were seeing someone new ... This Amy. It seems like you're into her a whole lot."

"I am," I admit before I can stop myself. "I'm in deep shit, guys," I tell them. "I can't stop thinking about her, and it's killing me."

"You love her?" Jay asks.

"Who is this Amy?" Chase raises a brow as he questions.

"I..." I stop because I wonder if I can answer that question. If I want them to even know. It is blunt, and it makes my heart tumble, leaving me breathless. I decide these are my guys. They are family. I have to tell someone. I need someone on my side or someone who will call me out.

"She's Lucas's sister, guys," I confess. "She's that Amy, and I can't get her out of my head."

18

———

AMY

Poking myself with a needle, I groan from the pain.

"Maybe you should take a break?" Casey suggests when she looks up from the sketch pad in front of her. "You've been at that for hours. Don't your neck and feet hurt?"

"They do," I reply, dropping on the bench behind me. "I think I need to sleep for weeks."

After the runway show and my one-week resting break, I only got busier. I'm designing a wedding dress for a celebrity model's wedding, and I need it to be just as amazing as Mika's.

"Cara's been on my neck all week. She wakes me up with the same message, 'No Mistakes, Amy love'."

"Cara's a self-centered bitch. You don't have to kill yourself over that, Amy. We both know you're the best in this and you'll get the job done, but you need a break."

Leaving her seat, Casey comes to me. Putting her hands on my shoulders, she massages a little, adding, "You can't afford to over-work right now."

"I know," I tell her.

Truth is I need to stay physically active, so my mind does not wander. I don't want to think of anything else but myself and my baby right now, but at intervals, Dylan and his confusing text enter my mind and it makes me wonder.

Calling him that night was a mistake. I was feeling really down and hormonal and I hadn't been able to stop myself. I was going to tell him the truth. Stupid, I know. So, in a sense, I'm glad he hung up on me. I kicked myself the whole rest of the night and the following day, only to get a text from him that night. And my heart hadn't stopped pounding since then.

Does this mean he cares? He loves me? Does he still want me?

I had seen his interview with Sawyer Fischer. He had been clear when he said he had no romance blooming, and no one special. It hurt to know he thought so little about what we had shared, but it gave me the confirmation I needed that he was really over me. That it really was time to move on. But then that damned text came, confusing me completely.

Celebrities lie on camera all the time; the interview doesn't count. But do texts?

Subconsciously, I'm still waiting for another text from him, or a call, and each time my phone buzzes, a part of me bounces, hoping that it's Dylan, only to drop with disappointment when I realize it's someone else.

Removing her hands from my shoulders, Casey comes to stand in front of me. "I'll continue from here, you should go grab something to eat," she suggests.

"I don't feel like it yet," I say, moving back on the bench so I can admire the dress I'm designing. "This lace is exquisitely expensive, and the crystals make it seem surreal. I'm sure Cara will love this."

"Of course, she will. You are a genius at this, Amy, don't doubt yourself."

Casey grins at me after the compliment, and I'm a bit relieved because of her constant support and cheering up. Turning my head, I stare at my phone on the table again.

Will he call? Will he text?

I wish I could talk to him and tell him about my recent accomplishments while sharing his. After watching his interview and seeing the massive support he had from his fans on social media concerning his foundation 'Hearts-WithYou', I know Dylan is going to succeed with it.

There are already a lot of people signing up for the platform. The official social media account page has over a million followers already, and it has only been a week since he talked about it.

"You're lost again," Casey says. "You know what? I'll order take-outs. I know you love Thai food, so I'll get you fried chicken wings, and rice."

The order arrives after thirty minutes, and I eat with Casey while discussing some emails I got asking me to collaborate with another top brand for their summer collection.

"We have an entire catalog of designs you worked on some time last year, do you remember? We can improve on that and pitch it to them, what do you think?"

Taking another bite of chicken wings, she smiles as I nod my agreement.

As I get home from my studio office a bit later, I lie in bed, staring at my ceiling for a while. My phone rings and I jump to pick it up only to see that it's Lucas calling.

He's grinning widely when I stare at him and force on a smile.

"How's it going, little sis?" he asks. As he moves around,

I see he's with his friends. "Just wanted to check in on you. Mika's in New York with Mom and they'll come see you tomorrow."

"That's great," I say. A brief glimpse of Dylan when Lucas moves his phone around again shows him taking down two shots of his drink.

"What's happening?" I ask Lucas. "I've been working my brains off recently, and I need to cool off."

"You should. We're leaving for LA tomorrow," he announces. "Our tour ends in New York, so I may be able to come see your show. Mom's talking about you a lot these days, it's like you're her new favorite."

Laughing at his joke, we go on talking for a short time before he says goodbye so he can get back to partying with his friends. When I close my eyes to fall asleep later, my heart is a bit settled and I think it's because I caught a glimpse of Dylan.

He didn't look so happy, but he was well, and that is relieving for me.

I miss you, Amy. His text is lodged in my mind, and the words make my heart flutter a bit every time I remember them. *Don't kid yourself, Amy.* I don't want to hold unto false hope. It is better for my heart that I don't.

Wrapping my hands around my stomach, I sigh as I will my mind to shut down so I can fall asleep and shut Dylan out of my mind.

Shopping for materials the next day, I spend time browsing through fabrics, wanting the best from my dealers. Earlier, I sent out the catalog for my collaboration with the designers interested in a summer collection, and I am hoping for a positive outcome even while I work on Cara's wedding dress and a few other designs for my own collection. It's for next Summer and I'm calling it 'Bold n' Beautiful.'

It is a collection for pregnant women and post-partum women who are yet to get comfortable with the changes their bodies experience during pregnancy. Having noticed a few changes to my body already, I knew with each passing day, they would be more progressive.

Three weeks have passed since I learned out about my baby, and I am almost three months pregnant. My stomach is still small, but getting more rounded, and even though I'm not experiencing any morning sickness, the fatigue and heartburn are intense during the day.

Needing a second to relax, I pull a chair close to me and sit so Casey can do the rest of the bargaining. Once we finish placing our orders, she drives us to Keaton Designs studio, and I turn on the air conditioning once I walk inside because I fear I might be about to collapse from the heat.

"Is it just me?" I ask. "Or do you feel this heat wave?"

Casey shrugs. "Your body's different from mine right now, so I don't feel it's that hot, but it's summer anyway, so you might be right. Will ice cream help?"

"I think so."

Casey orders my favorite butterscotch and chocolate chip cookie dough ice cream, and having finished the large-sized cup she got me in less than ten minutes, I move to sit close to her so I can have some of hers. Casey and I start going about her new love interest, the man she married while we were in Hawaii.

"He's still refusing to give you a divorce?" I ask, and she nods.

"It's crazy, and honestly, I don't think I can say no anymore because I kind of like him."

"He's hot?" I ask, and she nods, giving me a sheepish grin.

"He's damn hot," she replies, getting us giggling like school kids for a full second before going back to discussing work again.

By evening, Mika and my mother come over, taking me out for a fun night at a rooftop restaurant and bar where they have karaoke. Thoughts of Dylan's voice, and the smile it brings to my lips whenever he sang invade my mind.

Taking the mic after my mom, Mika sang for a long time before handing it back over to my mom. They make me sing a song before the end of the night and when they drop me off at home, I'm feeling a bit elated because it's the best fun I've had in a while.

By the end of the week, it's time to take Cara's wedding dress to her house for the final fitting with Casey. I'm excited to see her reaction, but also dreading it at the same time.

Working with Casey in Cara's well-furnished living room, I'm surprised when Cara puts on the TV and starts watching the entertainment news station where Soul Sounds is performing their concert in Oregon. The tour started a little over a month ago and since they have almost two months left, they are going to come up on the news several times.

Cara is obviously a fan because she is singing along to their lyrics without missing a single word, and Casey joins her. My eyes wander occasionally to the TV, but I fight the urge to just stare hoping to catch a glimpse of Dylan.

After the brief news replay, we go on singing their

album Cara decides to play and working on her final fitting to make sure every angle of the dress is superb.

Turns out Cara isn't as horrible as Casey and I thought even though she is quite demanding, and she hosts us for the night with drinks and a meal prepared by her Italian chef. My yummy alfredo pasta seafood serving gets demolished, and since my appetite is larger these days, dessert soon follows.

As we get an invitation to the wedding, and since it's being held on a yacht, Cara sends a pick-up to get us in the morning.

The ceremony is beautiful and peaceful too. There's a lot of media coverage and Cara gives me a thumbs up in front of her audience when she's asked to give a little speech about how she's feeling.

Social media is raging with comments on my work by the end of the weekend, and by Monday morning, there are numerous requests for interviews and features in top magazines.

"We might need to hire some employees soon," Casey says when I arrive at the studio that morning with Pizza and ice cream. Cravings are a bitch. "An assistant, some designers to join the team, preferably interns in the fashion industry, and a support team worker to help with menial errands and keep stock."

Taking a bite of my pizza, I start humming to myself, laughing when she looks at me and arches a brow. "Are you eating without me?"

"Of course not," I reply, taking another mouthful bite. "Come join me."

"I will, we need a full tummy for work today," she says, sitting beside me so we can empty the pizza pack.

After eating, it's back to work on new designs for my

summer catalog, and by mid-afternoon, I get the email from the fashion line to whom I submitted a catalog.

"We're officially going to Paris," I announce after reading their deal and collaboration email inviting us to work with them at the Paris Fashion Week.

Looking shocked, Casey's face lights up as she squeals with excitement.

19
———————

DYLAN

Hanging out with my friends lately is awkward because Jay and Chase know my secret, but I've yet to tell Lucas about Amy.

After our last concert in Oregon, we are resting for the week before traveling to Los Angeles for an open-mic concert where some of our fans will be allowed to climb the stage and join the performance.

As Ken works on the details for the open-mic, I'm practicing my notes for the next concert. Walking into the studio room where I'm sitting with Jay and Chase who are, for once, quietly fiddling with their phones, Lucas flops on the chair before he puts his hand on Jay's shoulder and asks, "What's up?"

"Ken is supposed to meet with us," Jay replies. "I want to know what he thinks of my new baby."

"What baby?" Chase asks.

Dropping my guitar, I'm curious so I have to move close to my guys to see what Jay is showing them on his phone. Lucas breaks into laughter first before he asks, "You call the car a baby?"

"It's a real babe," Chase comments, then takes the phone and starts to admire the sleek ride Jay purchased.

Talks start about the car, and how much Jay spent before he could swap his last one. Lucas goes on about the gift he got Mika for the wedding, and there's a lot of laughter when I join in and mention the sports car Ken got and bashed some weeks before the tour began.

It's a light-hearted moment made better when Ken comes in and shares the news on the plans for our biggest concert ever, the open-mic will be in The Novo- Downtown LA, and I am already anticipating the event even, though it's still a week away.

That evening, hanging out at a club, we are celebrating our last day before heading for LA in restricted area with a few others inside the VIP section. Jay is lost somewhere on the dance floor with some woman while Chase is working with the DJ to make sure the entire place stays booming.

Caught in my head, I sit in silence for a long time, and Lucas, on his second bottle of beer while I am on my fifth shot, is right by my side keeping as quiet as me. Not yet feeling numb in the slightest, I order another and down it.

"How you been, man?" Lucas breaks the silence. "The foundation is getting a lot of attention now; Ken tells me you've even had some clinical psychiatrists volunteer to work in some states where you want centers established."

I nod. "Yes, everything is happening really fast. And it's bigger than I ever dreamed of. I mean, think of all the people who could potentially benefit from this."

"True," Lucas agrees. "I'm proud of you, man. You got it done," he says with a wistful smile. "Remember when we were playing at that back-alley club in San Jose? Who would have thought we would become popular worldwide?"

"I know," I answer, then shake my head. "We did it!"

As Lucas grins at me, I can't hold back my smile. This guy is my closest friend and the first I got close to, the first I ever opened to about my life when we were younger. Although he already played with Chase and Jay at the club, they needed a guitarist, so it was easy for me to join the team.

"We've come a long way, man, and I think I'm prouder of you than anyone else. You put a lot of passion and soul into our band ... All of us do, but I understand where yours stems from, and it also serves as a motivation for me."

Lucas's words make the guilt hammering at me for a while now intensify. Averting my eyes from the intensity of his stare, Amy slips into my mind, and how she made me promise not to tell Lucas.

"I'm sorry, Amy," I whisper to myself.

"What was that?"

Swallowing hard, I look him in the eye and say, "I had sex with Amy."

As he blinks, the corner of Lucas's lips curves into a shaky smile. "I don't understand."

"We had a fling while we were in Hawaii," I continue. "But I ended things before leaving. I've wanted to tell you that for a while now, and I just ... I didn't want you to get mad."

Getting to his feet, Lucas turns away from me quietly. Following his lead, I get up too, so I can follow him if he walks away. *This conversation needs to happen. He needs to understand...* Pain slices through me. My whole face is screaming from his fist. My balance is off, so tilting backward, I land on the table behind me and crash it into pieces. I'm a bit stunned by the pain and the fall, but he isn't done yet. Grabbing me by my shirt, Lucas hurls me back up, then punches me in the face again and the pain is almost crushing this time. "She's my little sister, you piece of ..."

I guess the shock of having Jay drag him away as his arm is already poised for another blow stops him from swearing. I'm too stunned to do anything, but I feel like I deserved those blows. Stepping back, I wipe my lips with my thumb. My nose is aching and so is my jaw as I rotate it.

"I'm sorry, Lucas," I say in a loud voice as he struggles with Jay to try and come at me again. I knew he would kill me, but I had to be honest with him. Whenever thoughts of her weren't consuming me, the guilt would crush me. He is my best friend and I was lying to him.

"You told him?" Chase asks, shock clear in his voice.

"You knew about this?" Lucas yells angrily, renewing his efforts to come at me again, but Jay has him restrained steadily.

Getting back into the VIP section, Ken takes in the scene. "What the hell do you think you're doing?" he shouts.

Lucas doesn't say a thing as he turns, forcefully releasing from Jay's hold, and storms out. Jay and Chase's disapproving looks as they walk away speak volumes. Ken is still staring at me in confusion.

"What just happened? Why did Lucas hit you?"

"I don't want to talk about it," I say, walking out of the bar too.

Next time I see either of my friends is when we board our private jet for LA. The silence in the cabin is oppressing as our attention seems focused on different things. Social media is raging about my fight with Lucas at the club, but no one is asking or saying anything including Ken, who just stares hard at me.

·   ·   ·

I S THIS END FOR THE S OUL B ROTHERS?

Social Media rages as Lucas, the lead singer of the Soul Sounds, rams his fist into his brother's face.

N EWS REPORTS ON TV ABOUT OUR EPISODE HAVE THE rumors of us disbanding, which are now trending on every social media outlet.

What happens to the foundation? Will they perform in LA? How do we explain the fight between men who have been best friends for over a decade? Whose side are Jay and Chase on? Does it even matter?

The trip to LA is a whopping fourteen hours with an extra forty-one minutes and I feign sleep the entire time. As we arrive at our five-bedroom penthouse, I go into one of the rooms, locking myself in until Ken knocks on my door some hours later.

"Are you going to tell me what's gotten into you two?" he asks, sitting on the chair in my room and crossing his legs.

"Not really in the mood."

"You don't have a choice. This is bad for the image of the band and your foundation. If you two don't work this out publicly, no one is going to trust the ..."

"Lucas and I don't have an issue. We can sort this out on our own, I just need to talk to him."

"Then what happened?" Rubbing a hand over my jaw, I press my lips together, not wanting to give Ken the details about our rift. Of course, it's not like I have a choice, like he said. "Fine ... I had a thing with his sister, and he got mad about it."

"You did what?" Ken asks in shock. "Dylan, how could you..."

"She's an adult, okay? It's not like I seduced her or something."

"She's his sister, and you are..."

As I arch a brow, Ken trails off.

"I'm what? Too old? Not good enough? A player? Not deserving? Come on, Ken, tell me what I am?" I throw at him. "This is stupid," I say, getting on my feet to walk out of the room, as the door bursts open, and Lucas walks in.

Face tight in a frown, his eyes stay on Ken. "I want to perform solo for the open-mic."

"What?" Ken jerks to his feet. "Lucas, you're insane."

"Lucas..." I begin, not wanting him to make a reckless decision because of what happened between Amy and me.

"Stay out of this," he sneers at me.

"Lucas, I can't let you do that because that only fuels the rumors of disbandment. Is that what you want? You want out?"

His silence hurts as he doesn't answer immediately. As I try to reach out to him again, he says. "She's my sister, Dylan."

"I know, and I'm sorry. It was a fling, I didn't mean for it to happen, but it did, and I'm sorry."

Lucas scoffs. "You're sorry? You ended things with her and you're sorry?" He looks me in the eye as he adds, "Don't you know that makes it worse? Why would you do a thing like that?"

"Lucas ..."

"She's my little sister, damn it, and you could just do that? Then sit there and act like you're my friend?"

"I *am* your friend."

"Lucas, let's take a moment to think about this for the sake of the band and ..."

"Fine!" His eyes turn to Ken. "Have it your way. I'll do it for the sake of the band, but I don't think I can stand him right now."

Lucas walks out of my room after that, and Ken looks me in the eye. "Fix this," he says, pointing to the door from where Lucas just stormed out before he storms out too.

Dropping onto my bed, I close my eyes again. My temples are pounding, my chest is tight, and it feels like I will lose control of my breathing soon because the pressure building is crushing me.

My phone rings at some point, and I'm relieved to take the call from my dad.

"What's happening, Son? You and Lucas?"

"I'm sorry, Dad," I say, feeling like I need to apologize for ruining everything just when it was starting to become so much more. "Lucas is threatening to leave the band. I don't think I can do anything to stop him unless he forgives me."

"What happened between you two? Is it fixable?"

Amy's love confession assaults me as every memory of our time together comes flooding back to me. Her smile, her scent, the moistness of her lips, the way her body feels against mine. The tenderness of her touch when she's close to me, the kindness in her eyes when I talk to her.

"I think I love her," I reply to my dad, not realizing what I'm saying until I hear him gasp.

"You love Mika? You fought because of her?"

"What? No! Dad, come on, how can you think that?" I ask, panicking as I sit up on my bed, rubbing my forehead some more. "No, not Mika, I would never do that to a friend."

"Oh, that's relieving," he replies and giggles a bit. "You're in love, Son, that's a good thing."

"Is it? Lucas is mad at me and I'm about to lose everything but all I can think about is her ... Amy, Lucas's little sister. She is all I can think about. Has been since the wedding in Hawaii."

"Then make it right, Son. I know you can make it right," he says. "You just need to figure out how."

20

———

AMY

I'm hyper-active the entire week at the Paris Fashion Show. My designs rock the runway, there are a lot of comments from the attendees about how good I am in the field and the recommendations keep flowing in.

I'm even doing a photo shoot for Vogue's cover before leaving Paris, and Casey is working with the make-up team to give me a bright look.

"I need more contour and focus on her tone, remember what we told you, we don't want anyone noticing the changes," she instructs Jean who joined my team of artists after we worked together in New York.

"She's cranky, non?" Jean comments when Casey leaves us in the dressing room for a while.

"She's nervous and so am I." I chuckle, getting quiet as some models enter the dressing room.

"It seemed intense," one of them says. "I wonder what they're fighting about, and I hear it's leading to disbandment, neither of them said anything to the media and social media is raging. There's a fan page about the entire thing."

"What thing?" I ask, interrupting their conversation

even though I know it's rude. "I'm sorry, I just overheard ... What are you talking about?"

"Didn't you hear? Two members of Soul Sounds got into a fight in Oregon, it was intense."

With shaky hands, I accept the tablet the model hands over and watch the video. My heart lurches painfully in my chest as Lucas hurls Dylan to his feet only to punch him hard in the face.

Jean gasps. "Oh Lala ... That was a hard one," he comments.

Replaying the video twice, I sigh before returning the tablet to the model and thanking her. "Could we wrap this up quickly, Jean? I need to make a call."

"Sure thing, ma perle," he replies, continuing with what he's doing to my face.

Squeezing my hands in fists, I attempt to stop the uncontrollable tremors that've taken them over. My throat constricts, and my mouth is dry. What could they be fighting about?

Lucas is never one to get in a fight, and though Dylan is generally grumpy, it didn't seem like he would pick one either. Racking my mind for a plausible cause for their rift, it finally dawns on me.

Could it be? ... Did Lucas find out?

Mika is the one person I can call to find out, and as soon as Jean is done with my make-up, hurrying out of the dressing room into the toilet, I take out my phone.

She picks on the first ring, sounding exhausted. Yawning, she says, "I'm in L.A, just landed, and gosh, it feels like my eyes will pop out any minute now if I don't sleep."

"Mika, I'm sorry ... Is Lucas alright? Dylan too? What's happening in L.A?'

Her silence freaks me out for a couple of seconds, until

she says, "Lucas is upset, I haven't seen him yet, but when we spoke earlier, he mentioned he was leaving the penthouse where he's supposed to stay with the rest of his friends. He says he can't stand them. Your mother met with Ken immediately after we landed, and I don't know what they discussed yet, but things do not look good."

"I think this is about me," I say, pacing around the small space in the toilet. "God, what do I do?"

"This is not your fault and there is nothing you *can* do," Mika says. "Let the boys sort it out."

"The band means a lot to them; I can't let them throw it all away. If they are fighting because Lucas found out about Dylan and me, then...."

"Don't stress over it," Mika repeats. "Let them sort it out, honey. You're not going to be able to do much from Paris right now, so they've got to figure it out on their own."

Mika's words make sense, but they don't help. Or maybe my worry is aggravated because of the pregnancy hormones always messing with how I feel.

"When Lucas gets to you, I need to talk to him. He won't take my calls, I know, but just help me out, okay?" I plead.

"Alright, dear."

Ending the call, I suck in a deep breath to steady myself before going back out to get dressed for my photoshoot. The entire time the camera lights flash in my face, I'm forcing my smile to stay on for them.

This shoot needs to be perfect because it's my first Vogue shoot, but at the same time, my heart won't stop racing, and my worry won't subside.

Being too busy to go on social media, Casey hasn't seen the news yet, so, the second we are done with the shoot and on our way home, I confess everything to her, starting with, "I'm pregnant with Dylan's baby."

Shocked to silence, it takes a couple of excruciating minutes to come up with, "Dylan, Dylan? Your brother's friend, Dylan?"

"Yes," I say, looking back into her eyes. "No one knows this, but I think Lucas knows we had a thing and he's mad about it."

"Damn," she exclaims. "What will you do?" she asks after a while.

"I don't know," I tell her, closing my eyes and covering my face with my hands. "I have no idea, honestly, but it wasn't just a fling for me, and when he ended it the way he did, I ... I've not been able to get over him yet."

Putting her hand over mine, she gives me a warm smile. "You'll figure it out, don't worry," she encourages.

<hr>

It's the next evening before I can get on a call with Mika and Lucas. He is grumpy as he looks at me while rubbing his face continuously.

"I'm sorry, Luc... I should have told you," I say in a solemn voice.

"Told me what? That you were sleeping with my best friend?"

"It wasn't just sex; you have to know that," I quickly add. "I fell in love with him, Lucas, and I knew what I was getting into. I know he's rough around the edges, and I know he's your best friend and you've known him longer than I do, but Dylan's a great guy, and I fell for him. He tried pushing me away, but it didn't work for either of us, so it wasn't entirely his fault."

Lucas is quiet for a long time, but he doesn't take his eyes off the screen.

"I don't want to be the reason you guys separate; I'll never forgive myself."

"It has nothing to do with you," Lucas says. "He's my best friend and you're my little sister. He should have known better than to..."

"I not a little girl anymore," I point out softly. "I made a choice, and I can't let you get mad at Dylan over it. What we had ended in Hawaii, and we haven't been in contact since then, but I'm alright ... I'm happy and I'm doing well."

"Are you?" he asks me as his brows furrow. "You said you fell for him, and then you ended things." I stay silent.

"That son of a ..." Lucas starts to curse when I give him a sad smile, but he stops himself. "Did he reject you? Is that why he ran off first? Because he was too scared to love you too?"

"I know his history, Lucas, and I understand him. You don't have to tell him anything or say anything about me. You just need to forgive him for my sake, and the band's too, please."

I hope my plea softens my brother's heart. A bad reputation is not what the band needs at this time, and I can't be the factor in their demise.

They've come a long way, and Dylan just started fulfilling his dreams of running the foundation. If they end it now, he might not be able to keep the fanbase he has.

"It's alright," Lucas says. "I just need you to not make choices that make you cry, Amy. You act tough but I know you get hurt easily. And Dylan acts tough too, but deep down, he's just a guy who's never experienced what love could really feel like. I know these things, but I got mad because I thought he played you and hurt you."

"That's not what happened, believe me," I say as I remember the passion Dylan and I shared. "It's my first time loving someone like this, Lucas, and I really just want him to be happy right now. The band does that for him. He needs it more than he needs anyone or anything else."

Lucas sighs and shakes his head. "I've got to go," he says. "I guess I have to apologize for hitting him now."

I chuckle and he smiles at me before he waves and ends the call. My chest feels lighter after the call with Lucas, as I walk into my bedroom in the suite I'm sharing with Casey and Jean.

After a hot shower, standing in front of my mirror, I stare at my body. Putting a hand on my abdomen, turning to the side so I can look at my side view, I admire the curve of my growing bump.

I'm about to start my second trimester. So far, my body is adjusting, I don't feel so tired anymore, and there isn't much dizziness and weakness, but there are cravings and headaches.

My heart tingles as I think of how the rest of my pregnancy will be.

What will he or she look like? Will it resemble Dylan? Have his eyes and smile?

It's still too soon to know, but maybe during my next ultrasound.

I go to bed that night thinking of Dylan, but it isn't the usual thoughts that fill me with an ache. I'm happier, so I think maybe I'm starting to accept the fact that we will never be together, and there is nothing I can do to change that.

He made a choice. My life is completely different now. I'm having a baby, his baby, and I'm doing better than I anticipated in my career.

I can be happy this way even though I miss him. I know I can, and that thought alone is encouraging.

The next morning, while I prepare for the last day of the Paris Fashion Week, Casey runs into my room. "Have you seen the news?" she asks me with wide eyes and an enthusiastic smile.

"No, what?" I ask, my pulse jumping because of her excited tone.

"We're a full clothing line collaboration with another major A-List fashion brand, and they want us to lead their summer collection runway designs. I just saw their email, and I can't believe it."

"This is insane," I say, getting on my feet.

"Right now, we need to celebrate," Casey suggests. Following her out of my room, she grabs a bottle of fruit wine since I'm not supposed to take any alcohol. Jean joins us for the quick toast and my joy in that moment skyrockets.

"To everything we've wished for and more," Casey toasts.

"To Keaton's" I add, clinking glasses with her and Jean.

I can't wait to see what the next chapter of my success holds for me.

21

———

DYLAN

MY FATHER ARRIVES IN LA A DAY AFTER WE DO, AND I'm at the airport to pick him up. As we arrive at the suite where my friends and I are staying, I take him into the guest room I already had Ken set up for him. It is his first time attending any of my concerts in person, and even though chances are that we won't perform, I am still excited to have him around.

"How's it going?" he asks with a smile as we settle him in his room. Sitting on his bed, facing him, he adds, "How's it with Lucas? You two made up yet?"

Shaking my head, I sigh. "I don't want to talk about it yet, Dad."

He looks at me for a long while before saying, "I think you should try talking to him, though."

"I've tried." And I have, yesterday, but he didn't give me a chance before he left the suite. And he hasn't come back yet. Chase and Jay are also giving me the silent treatment. They act like it's not their concern, but the judgmental look in their eyes says otherwise.

"I hate that this is even a problem ... It shouldn't be, but I don't know what got over me."

"Did you really fall in love with her?" my dad asks. He must be remembering our phone conversation.

"Yes. No. I don't know." I'm all over the place, going back and forth on this issue. "I don't even think love exists, Dad. I've never experienced it or know what it feels like, so how can I say one way or the other?"

"It's a wonderful feeling, Son, I can tell you that," he replies, putting his hand over mine. Staring at our joined hands, I raise my eyes to his.

"What about when it ends? What if it doesn't work out? I would hate to regret hurting her or getting hurt by her. I mean, look at you and mom. How do I survive that if it ends that way? It would kill me if I loved someone and lost them."

Eyes softening, he shakes his head before he says, "Not all relationships end that way. Your mom and I ..." He shrugs. "We fell apart, and we fell out of love, but it doesn't mean that it ends that way for everyone else." Looking into my eyes, he adds, "When you love someone, you'll do everything to make it work, and if you need to let them go, you'll do that. It'll be fine, and you'll be alright because you love them."

"It would hurt."

"Yes, it would, but at least you'd know you tried."

Falling silent again, I release a deep breath. "So, you think I should tell Lucas this? I should tell him I fell for his sister?"

"Yes." He is nodding. "You should definitely tell him."

A soft knock comes on my door before Ken steps in before either my dad or I can say anything. After greeting my dad, Ken faces me. "There's an interview for you tomorrow," he tells me. "It should be you and Lucas on it. Have you worked out your problems?"

As I remain silent, his disappointment is clear in his eyes. "I told you to fix it," he reminds me.

"He's not even speaking to me, and I haven't seen him since last night."

"Fix it," Ken states again before he leaves my dad's room.

As my dad chuckles for a bit, I smile at him before heading out to my room. The rest of the day I work on perfecting my notes on the guitar. The open mic performance is our first concert here and our biggest so far and I need it to go down in history as Soul Sounds' best.

We need to put in our best, and we can't do that if we aren't even on speaking terms.

Worrying about Lucas and the rest of the band, by evening, I decide to go find Jay and Chase so we can talk. They are in the living room when I come out of my room.

As I join them with a can of beer in one hand, Jay glances at me briefly, before returning his focus to the game he's playing.

"I need to talk to you," I say. "Both of you," I add so I can get their attention.

Jay and Chase were friends before they met Lucas, and when I joined the band, the four of us easily formed a bond because we all have something in common. We love music, even if we all express it differently.

"What's up?" Jay asks while Chase quietly watches us both.

"I'm sorry ... Everything happening right now is on me, but it was never my intention to hurt Amy, and it still isn't."

When neither of them speaks, I continue, summoning the courage to say the words I never thought I would say.

"I fell in love with her, guys. I love her ... I think Amy is the one for me."

Chase blinks as Jay bursts into a short laugh and jokes. "Our friend is a lost man."

I join in the laugh because, for the first time, Jay's joke is right, and I shake my head.

"I am," I say. "I am completely in love with her, and I don't know what to do about it."

"There's nothing you can do," Chase, always the romantic, says smiling as he pats my shoulder. "You just need to feel it, and fix things with Lucas."

"Yeah," Jay adds, serious for once. "You guys, with Mika and Amy, are all the family I have, and I never want us to fight again."

"You guys and my dad are my family too. Don't worry, bro. I'll fix it," I say with determination, reaching for my phone in my pocket to call Mika. She's the one person who can help me get through to Lucas.

I'M AT THE STUDIO WAITING TO BE INTERVIEWED WITH White Papers, a notorious gossip column in Los Angeles. Excited but also nervous, I'm happy Jay and Chase are at the venue with me, but Lucas is yet to arrive.

When I contacted Mika yesterday, she hadn't put Lucas on the phone because he wasn't with her. I tried calling her a few times after that, but she didn't take the call either. I am hoping with all my heart that Lucas shows up for the interview.

This is all we've worked hard for, man; I think as I pray silently that he shows. *Let's not throw it all away.*

It's a few minutes to the interview when Mika and Lucas walk in. My heart lightens immediately, and I hurry toward them, smiling at Mika.

"Thanks for showing up," I tell Lucas. "I'm so sorry about everything."

He nods. "This band and the foundation are important to me too. I won't let anything screw it up."

His steady smile warms my heart and there is no time for us to talk about anything else, so we go right into the interview first.

It's a three-hour show, and the entire time, Lucas and I talk about the start of Soul Sounds, and the foundation. Jay and Chase join in after the first one hour because that is the set-up the interview Michael Walters wants, and it becomes more fun when he asks more personal questions about us as individuals.

After the interview, Lucas, Mika, Ken, and my dad ride with me for dinner at a five-star restaurant Lucas booked for us.

While eating, I'm quiet the entire time. A lot is going through my mind, and most of it is about Amy.

How is she doing? Now that I know how I feel, I no longer want to deny it. She's important to me, and she makes my heart flutter. It's a brand-new feeling ... Exciting and intoxicating. I am craving her now more than ever, and it's leaving a breathless feeling inside me.

I want to tell her. It's the only thing I can think of doing, and imagining what her expression will look like makes me shiver. It won't be easy to win her forgiveness, but I want to try. I have to. All those things keeping us apart before seem so small compared to what I feel inside.

Throughout the entire time, Jay jokes about Ken's outfit for the photoshoot we're having tomorrow, and I join the laughter around the table.

It's amazing how much lighter and freer I am just by accepting my feelings. As we finish eating, all I can think about is talking to Lucas, so I ask him to come out with me, and we drive off to another bar. Ordering a double scotch and single malt for myself as he has a tequila, we both take our first shot before I start.

"I'm sorry about Amy."

Lucas nods before he looks at me. "She's my sister, but you're my brother," he says. "You're just as important to me as she is, you should know that."

"I love her, Lucas," I tell him, bracing myself for another rage from him. "I know you think it shouldn't. I should treat her like my sister too, but she's more than that to me. I fell in love with her, and it's crazy coming from me, I know, but that is how I feel. I'm in love with Amy and I want to tell her, but I need your blessing because you're my brother too... No matter what happens."

Lucas is quiet for a long time, and I feel a certain shiver deep inside me.

I don't want to be apart from Amy anymore because I've suffered her absence for too long. Asking for Lucas's blessing is because of who he is to us and because I respect him. I feel it is only natural that he feels protective over her.

"What if I say no?" he asks. And then it hits me. I care about what it thinks but...

"Either way, it won't stop me from going after her. But you are my best friend, my brother, my family, and I really want you to be okay with this. So, I ask again, do I have your blessing?" I'm curious about his answer, but this feeling of certainty is liberating.

"You have it," Lucas says after a while.

Blinking my shock away, I clear my throat. "You mean that?" I ask in a shaky voice.

"I know my sister, Dylan, and she isn't one to make the wrong choice in guys. If you love her, just promise me you won't hurt her ... Ever."

"I would never," I assure him with strong conviction. My feelings for Amy are intense and pure, and I need him to understand that.

"Then you've got my blessing."

We end the night with a hug, and the next day is our first performance in LA. We open with our newest song, 'Heal Me'. While I'm singing, all I think about is Amy. She is all I see, and I don't mind at all. For the first time in my adult life, I want something, and I'm happy to have it.

I don't care about my past; I don't care that I could get hurt, but I'm no longer worried about hurting her. I now know I would never again be able to. Hurting her would be like hurting me times one hundred. So, I am willing to try to make it work, and I'm hoping our love will last.

That night in my room, I try calling Amy. Waiting till her line connects takes me to voicemail. My heart sinks a little because I was hoping I could hear her voice before going to bed, but it doesn't discourage me in the least. I don't leave a message because what I have to say to her, I want to say as I look into her beautiful blue eyes.

Later, Mika lets me know Amy is in Paris on a fashion show, and I spend the next afternoon watching reels and video snippets of her runway show in Paris on social media.

Amy's talent is making waves in the fashion industry, and I am so proud of her.

All I want to do right now is speak to her, hear her voice,

see her smile, hug her, and spend time in her arms. Racking my brains for the perfect way to confess my feelings to her, an idea runs through my mind, but I need to run it through Ken first. Calling him, I ask for his location so we can meet up to plan.

22

AMY

Finishing my drink with Casey, I relax on my seat, closing my eyes for a second. The fashion week is over, and it's time to return to New York, but I need more time to myself here in Paris.

It's a beautiful city, and it feels like the last time I had fun was during Lucas's wedding.

My body is rapidly changing. Today, I realized that I can't fit into my regular jeans anymore because my waist is a bit wider, and my thighs are getting fuller. When I stare at my reflection in the mirror, it feels like I am a different person.

"What should we do today?" Casey asks, standing from her chair and walking to the balcony of our five-star presidential suite booked by the brand we worked with for the fashion week. "I wish I could spend my time at the pool," Casey continues. "Clad in a bikini of my problems or worries. Just me, my tequila or cocktail, and the lovely water."

I laugh at the image she paints and shake my head. "Lucky you don't have to worry about an unborn child," I say, cradling my tiny protruding stomach. "I think about this one all the time, and spontaneity just isn't for me right now."

"There are other things we can do," Casey says. "We can try French food and wine. Oh right, you can't have alcoholic wine. But we could do a cruise by night or an open-top bus tour of the city.... It'll be fun."

As amazing as Casey's ideas are, what I really want to do is sit by myself in this hotel and remember the time when I was the happiest. The smile on my face is a wistful one and she must notice it because she stops talking, coming to sit by my side.

"You miss him, don't you?" she asks.

I nod once, then sigh. "I do ... I really do."

Her arms envelop me. As much as I needed that, I need to get my mind off this path, so I lighten up the mood by taking her up on her suggestions. We end up going for a night tour in a vintage car with a local driver. His French accent makes it difficult to understand what he is saying half of the time, but it doesn't matter. I love the view, the tall buildings, and the city lights that brighten up the place even at night.

We drive past the Eiffel tower, then we have Beef bourguignon for dinner.

When I get back to the hotel, I'm exhausted, so I fall asleep and wake up to a text from Mika.

They made up ... Lucas and Dylan are performing a duet in Los Angeles this weekend and I think it'll be amazing if you're there.

. . .

After reading Mika's text, I go to Soul Sounds' fan page to see for myself. Taking advantage, I watch videos of their performance in LA and their interview with White Papers. Seeing Dylan's smile as he sings to the crowd makes my heart ache.

Tears form in my eyes and threaten to fall, and I hate that I am away from him at a time like this. My hand moves to my abdomen again and I stroke it gently.

It is for the best that it is just the two of us, little one. Maybe one day things will be different.

A part of me wishes he would come around, but so much time has passed now so I doubt it. It's difficult for me to let go of my love for Dylan, and I don't think it'll be possible for me to forget at all, especially now that I am having his child.

My second ultrasound is in a few weeks, and I want my mom to be there. I wonder how it would be to have Dylan there and I know I'd really love that. The entire night, I play with the idea of telling Dylan about the baby. I tried calling him before, but he hung up on me after I told him I missed him. All he said was he was sorry, but I have no idea what he is sorry for. Leaving me? Staying away? Being with me to begin with?

My mind is in turmoil, and it worsens watching his interview with White Papers, and his emotional talk about wanting to share love with the world. I always knew Dylan is a man capable of love, I can hear it in the way he speaks, and even his actions when we were together, but I know he is scared, and that fear will keep us apart because love is a conscious decision to give yourself to a person.

I wish things were different.

Our flight to New York is booked for two days from

now, and I spend the remaining time in Paris weighing my options. I could go to Los Angeles to see Dylan myself.

But what if he doesn't want anything to do with me?

My brother is also there, and I miss him too, so that's reason enough to go right there. Besides, I need closure from us one way or another. And the last thing I want to do is trap him into being with me with a child. Even if I go to Los Angeles, I still can't tell him about the baby. He doesn't want one and I'll never be happy if he is with me out of duty and obligation. The pull to see him is strong, as are my reasons to stay away, so my mind is a mess.

In the end, we return to New York, and Dylan's tour continues. I watch most of his shows on TV or online, and every one of them is magical, even the open mic.

Time rolls by slowly for me, and every day is uneventful because all I do is work, and rest. It's the end of the month soon, and I'm preparing for another show for my brand's second collection.

At my second ultrasound with my mom, seeing a live picture of my baby reminds me of how real my new life is.

"I'm going to be a mother soon," I tell her with tears in my eyes as she holds my hand in the ultrasound room.

"And you'll be a great one, Amy, you have nothing to worry about," she assures me.

It's a touching moment, but it gives me courage. With time, every other piece of my life will fall back in place, and I'm certain that I'll be happy, eventually.

IT'S THE LAST DAY OF MY FASHION SHOW RUNS FOR A week, and I'm once again standing backstage watching the last set of models about to take the stage, while Casey is doing the instructing and organizing. Hands in the pockets of the coat I'm wearing, I'm wondering how all of this became possible for me.

Lost inside my mind and swallowed by the exhilarating feeling that floods me, I'm brought back to reality by Lucas's singing voice.

At first, I don't understand what's happening, but when I turn around, I see him standing there with Jay, Chase, Mika, and my mother.

"Surprise," he sings as I burst into a loud laugh, shocked that he is here.

"Oh God, how did you make it?" I ask, rushing toward Lucas and hugging him tightly. Closing my eyes, I soak in the happiness of knowing he is here with me. "I didn't know if you were coming to the show," I say, releasing him to hug Jay and Chase who congratulate me.

Lucas mentioned earlier that they were ending their tour here in New York, but I wasn't expecting to see them till later in the week.

As my eyes travel through the people in front of me, they land on Dylan behind them. His grin leaves me breathless for a second because, even though I have seen a lot of him on TV recently, seeing him in person still makes my heart stutter hard in my chest.

I step away from Chase, and that must be when Lucas has the chance to fully see me for the first time.

"You're pregnant?" His voice is loud and shocked. The dress I'm wearing is a bit tight, so my bump shows a bit, and the blazer I'm wearing over the dress isn't buttoned.

Silence descends all around us, and the grin on Dylan's face slowly fades. His eyes narrow a bit, still fixed on mine, and I immediately know that he's feeling the same shock and angst as Lucas.

I rub the back of my neck, not knowing what to say in that moment.

"I ... We should talk inside," I say to Lucas, but my eyes are on Dylan.

Lucas pales, as he turns around to look at Dylan. Everyone does the same. Dylan simply takes a step back, turning around, and hurries out through the door.

My heart sinks, and I have to release a deep breath because the downcast feeling swamping me is enough to bring me tears again.

"Amy..." Lucas starts.

"I'll go after Dylan," Chase says hurrying out, followed closely by Jay. Now it's just me, Lucas, Mika, and my mother.

At that moment, Casey comes backstage. "It's time for you," she says.

It's the end of the show, and I'm supposed to make the last appearance to say my appreciation to everyone.

"I need to ..." I say to Lucas.

"Go on, I'll be right here when you get back," he says, and my gratitude fills me as I turn and hurry away from them.

Forcing a smile and sucking in a deep breath to steady my insides, I climb onto the stage and walk forward to take the mic.

"Thank you, everyone," I begin, spending the next few minutes on my pre-prepared speech. There's a performance by a popular artist after my speech, and I escape backstage with Casey following me.

"Did something happen?" she asks in a hushed tone.

"Dylan came around," I explain. "He saw me ... He knows."

Her eyes widen, and I can tell she wants to talk about

this, but I don't have the time to say much to her, so hurrying away, I meet Lucas and Mika at the back again. They are waiting in a dressing room for me when I enter. Closing the door behind me, I rest my back against it for a bit.

"Yes, I am pregnant and it's Dylan's," I say, not wanting to waste any time on the issue. "I tried reaching out to him, but he didn't respond to my call. And after thinking this through and remembering our conversations, I was mostly decided on not telling him at all because I know he doesn't want kids, so I didn't want him to feel obligated to be with me because of the child."

"Oh Amy," Lucas says in a low tone, shaking his head. Closing his eyes, he rubs a hand over his face.

"I can do this on my own, you don't have to feel sorry for me," I say, confident in myself. My mom and Mika are quiet the entire time, and I add. "I know I can."

"It's not that," Lucas says as he gets on his feet. "Dylan has his issues ... He's had it rough from the start but he's a good guy still, and I think you should tell him; you don't have to do this alone."

"I don't want his pity."

"It's not about his pity, Amy," Lucas interrupts, shaking his head again. "He came here with me," he continues. "He came here, Amy ... to surprise you, with me. He wouldn't have done that if he didn't want to."

"What are you saying?"

"I'm saying you should talk to him," Lucas says, taking Mika's hand. "I love you, sis. Talk to Dylan," he adds, walking out of the dressing room.

Unable to move, I stand in the same spot for the next few minutes, and the sinking feeling in the pit of my stomach increases as I search my heart for the courage to face Dylan and look him in the eye, knowing that he doesn't want me.

Now that he knows about the baby, I'll just tell him everything I'm feeling.

He doesn't need to be a part of its life, or mine either. There's no choice to make.

23

______

DYLAN

Driving away from the venue of Amy's fashion show, the last thing I want to do is speak to anyone.

How could she keep this from me? A baby? She's having my baby.

My feelings are all over the place, but there's a sharp ache in my gut that almost makes me panic. My chest tightens, my breath is coming harshly, and I'm trying to work around the thoughts swimming through my mind.

The baby ought to be mine, right?

Judging from the look on her face when she saw me, and how Lucas responded with shock, I know deep down it is mine. I can't explain the conviction. The last time I saw Amy was four months ago. She isn't showing much yet, but the ball-sized extension of her abdomen is enough to show it.

Is it mine?

The doubt will continue eating at me, so instead of running, I decide to turn back around and confront her. Taking the next U-turn, I drive back toward the venue for the fashion show.

It's crowded on the red carpet out front, and I realize somehow the media has managed to corner Lucas and Mika, so they are stuck in the middle of the reporters, all crowding and asking questions.

Ken and some of our bodyguards approach the scene, probably trying to make out a way to rescue Lucas and Mika. Taking the back entrance we used to enter the hall earlier, I sneak in and don't stop walking till I get to the first dressing room. Amy isn't inside, and I check two other dressing rooms before I see her standing in the last one.

Stepping inside, I close the door behind me before she turns around and looks at me. She is pale, I hate that she looks sick. My heart pangs in pain again.

"Amy ..."

"I was going to tell you," she says, launching right into the conversation before I can say anything. "I called ... I tried. You didn't want anything to do with me, so you can't be upset that you didn't know."

"It's mine?" I ask even though it's not what I want to say. Still in shock, my mind is spinning in different directions. I was so sure of my feelings for Amy. I love her, I want her. It took me a long time to get this resolution. And now there's a baby on the way? I can't stop the panicked thoughts from clouding my judgment.

Will I be a good father? Is this even possible? What if it doesn't work out? I don't want to have a child grow up in the same environment that I did. It will make me just like my mother, and I have spent my entire life working to make sure I didn't make the same mistake my father did.

They say having a child changes you. My mother loved my father till she had me. What if the same happens with Amy? What if she starts resenting me for the child?

Closing my eyes for a bit, I re-open them to her intent

blue stare. The look in her eyes is a pained one, from the way her brows furrow, and how her lips quiver.

"I don't want to hurt you, Amy," I say, combing my fingers through my hair. "This is a bit too much for me to handle."

"I don't need you to handle this, or pity me," she says almost immediately. Before I can say anything else, she continues. "I'm handling this just fine on my own. We'll be fine with or without you, Dylan, so you don't have to be with me out of pity, and ..."

"Pity?" I stop her. "I'm not here because I pity you. I came here because..." I stop, sucking in a deep breath.

On my way here from the airport, I prepared a speech in my mind, wanting to tell Amy about my love for her, and everything I was feeling. How I thought about her every waking second of the day, and how every song I wrote for the past four months is about her.

"I came here to tell you that..." my voice trails off. My heart is pounding so loud in my chest and there is no way to calm it down because her eyes are intent on mine, reminding me of how intense her gaze can get. I breathe in deeply. Then out. I'm ready.

"I guess what I'm trying to say is that I'm in love with you, Amy, and I'm so sorry it took me this long to realize it."

She blinks, taking a step back. "I don't ... Dylan..."

"I love you, Amy," I repeat, gaining more courage this time. "I'm in love with you, and I want to be with you."

"Dylan, if this is because of the baby, then...."

"It's not," I say, shaking my head. "It really isn't. I came here to tell you that without even knowing about the baby, and I mean it. I know I have to win your trust back; I know you don't believe that I want this, but I need a chance ... I need a chance to prove it to you."

Amy is still quiet, hands are limp at her sides. Taking a step toward her, I reach for her hands, linking our fingers. Pulling her close to me, I tilt her chin a bit. She still doesn't resist me or say a thing. My head lowers next, about to kiss her. Stopping at the last second, I pull her into my arms for a hug instead.

"I missed you so much," I tell her, wrapping my hands around her waist as I suck in a deep breath to fill my nostrils and my core with a whiff of her scent.

She still doesn't move. As I move my hands down her back, she pulls away from me and steps back. "I need air," she says, hurrying out of the dressing room before I can stop her.

Running after her, I chase her out of the building through the back door, where she turns right, stopping when she reaches the side of the building. It's quiet there, but I can still hear the sounds coming from her event happening inside.

"Amy?" I call. "Are you alright?" My muscles tighten from the tears on her cheeks. Shaking her head, she looks at me and puts a hand on her chest. "I'm sorry, Amy," I say as I move closer to her.

She shakes her head. "I know, I'm just ... I don't know why I'm crying," she says amidst tears. "I'm happy ... I mean, it's surreal, but you're here, and I should be happy, but I'm crying too, and it's just crazy."

Sobs wrack out of her, and I can't bear watching, so going to her, I take her in my arms for another hug. This time, I don't release her till she stops. As she finally raises her head, I wipe her cheeks with my thumb.

"I've ruined your shirt," she says looking at me.

"I don't mind," I answer, pointing to the print on the shirt. "See? It says just that," I tell her. "And I really don't."

She's laughing, and I hug her again. I never want to leave her side, and I hope she gives me a chance to prove it to her. I came here with Lucas and the others because I was so anxious to see her, but my surprise visit is not over yet.

I have plans with Ken, but with how the day has been, I will have to make rearrangements.

My arms are still around Amy when my phone starts buzzing. "It's Lucas," I tell her. She moves away, and I take the call. "Hey man."

After learning I'm with his sister, Lucas asks us to meet them at the house here in New York where we're all staying for the end of our tour.

Our ride is silent, but I can't be apart from her yet, so I hold her hand tight the entire time. Lighting up every time I steal a glance, my smile is returned each time.

It's a full house when we arrive. Lucas, and the rest of my friends, Mika, who is with Amy's mom, and Casey, along with some of Amy's team workers.

Excited to see them, Amy hugs Casey and a tall, blond guy she introduces as Jean. After shaking his hand,

I join Chase and Jay where they are sitting.

"You two worked it out?" Chase asks me.

I nod, adding, "She's still in shock ... Processing, but I'll make sure she comes around."

"Ooooohhhhh, this is what love sounds like," Jay jokes as usual, and Chase, the romantic, smacks his shoulder as we all burst into full laughter.

Ken comes in last to join the hang-out, and he claps his hands to get everyone's attention.

"Dylan ... Jay," he calls because we're in the middle of a conversation still. Standing in front of everyone, he waits until I look at him, then announces, "We have an extra show."

"Show?" I ask, not fully understanding him.

"What show?" Lucas asks.

Every pair of eyes is on Ken, waiting. He grins wide, and adds, "We're having a private show for the Mayor's daughter's wedding. They want the band to perform at her wedding next weekend. It's perfect because it's a week before our last concert for this tour, and with the Mayor, your foundation has a huge success chance of getting more donations and findings."

My heart leaps with joy at the announcement, and Chase gets on his feet. "We should celebrate it, then," he announces, going into the kitchen. Never misses a chance, that one.

Turning to Amy, I find her looking at me with a sheepish smile on her face. Taking her hand in mine, I caress her fingers, then whisper, "I love you."

Blushing, she leans closer to me and responds, "I love you too."

Hearing her say the words makes my heart tingle. I realize I love the feeling, and I am drunk on it. How did it take me this long to realize?

I can't wait to tell my dad all about all I'm feeling, and I know he'll be excited for me. Even though I never considered myself the kind of man who would fall in love, he still believed.

That night, taking Amy to my room, I watch her get out of the dress she wore before handing her a T-shirt that reads, 'Craziness is my DNA'.

Putting it on, she lies on the bed beside me. Gathering her close, I make her head rest on my chest so I can feel the heat of her body.

We are quiet for a long time, the sounds of our breathing merged into one.

I am content and happier than I have ever been. *So this is what it feels like.*

I hope the euphoria never fades and lasts forever ... The longer I lie here enjoying her closeness the more I realize I really want it to last forever.

24

———

AMY

THIS IS PROBABLY A DREAM, BUT I LOVE IT. I DON'T mind that there's a crowd surrounding me, and everyone here is clamoring for a piece of Soul Sounds attention. I'm in the front row, but I'm still surrounded by a massive crowd cheering for Dylan and his friends.

Wearing a T-shirt that says, "Music for the Soul," I'm staring right at Dylan because he is the only one I see.

Singing the lyrics, I wave my hands in the air in sync with the others in the crowd. When they get to the hook of the song, Dylan plays his guitar, and it's amazing.

Getting up from his chair, he gives a full performance, stomping his foot on the ground to add more effect to it, and jumping when Lucas joins him to sing again.

At the end of the show, there's an open mic when they let the crowd do the singing. Jay and Chase continue playing, Dylan takes a break, waiting for his turn again before he joins and plays again.

Smiling wide as I watch the show, it feels good to be part of the large crowd.

As the show ends a couple of hours later, I get backstage. Humming one of their songs, I enter the dressing room where they are.

Dylan immediately comes to me, hugging me tight and kissing me thoroughly. Jay teases, "Get a room, you two."

Pulling away from Dylan, I blush furiously as Mika and Lucas laugh and Chase shakes his head. Keeping his hand around my waist, Dylan keeps me by his side.

"We should celebrate tonight," he announces.

Jay, a fun-lover who is always ready for a party, agrees by jumping on his feet. "Yes ... I have ideas."

As we all find our way out of the building, Dylan kisses the side of my neck and I smile at him. Getting into the waiting limo, we find Ken already inside, so we head for the spot Jay suggests.

That night, Dylan comes home with me. Lying in bed together, we enjoy the time we spend together. He tells me about his trip to the Mayor's daughter's wedding with his friends, and I already miss him even though he's still here.

He laughs at my joke about how boring it'll be without him.

Staying at my place for the rest of the week, Dylan is with me while I'm working on the designs for my summer collection.

That afternoon, while I'm obsessing about cuts and darts for a dress, he enters the room carrying a cup of fresh orange juice he got from a grocery store earlier. Handing it to me, he waits till I sip some of it before taking the glass from me again and dropping it on the table.

"Can I help with anything?" he asks.

"You don't like holding pins, do you?" I ask, remembering when I was working on Mika's wedding dress.

"I don't mind for you," he says.

"Smooth..."

Laughing, he takes the bowl of pins from the table and holds it in front of me so I can easily reach them.

For the next few minutes, I'm pinning the design I want on the fabric. "How is it?"

"Amazing," he replies. "Is this a dinner dress?"

"Yes, it could be."

"Is that what your summer collection is about?"

"Something like that ... It's more like summer-themed dinner dresses," I answer.

"Oh ... That's genius. We don't have to worry about you getting all hot and bothered while you are dancing or inside those stuffy event rooms."

I laugh. "It's perfect to be inside or outside. Sometimes, a lady still wants to go for a walk," I reply teasingly, then poke his shoulder a bit before he grabs me and pulls me to him for a kiss.

His body pressing against mine, I feel heat rising inside me till it pools between my thighs and makes me flush all over.

Backing me to the bed, I let him lower me before raising my head and meeting his kiss again. Stopping, Dylan breathes out deeply.

"I want to make love to you with everything in me," he says. His words make me burn hotter for him. Hooking my hands around his neck, I kiss him to silence.

"I want to make love to you too," I whisper, before parting my legs and wrapping them around his waist.

As he kisses me all over, I give in to the sensations coursing through me.

Our passion is hotter than the first time, and I don't want it to end. I crave Dylan ... I want to spend the rest of my life with him. He was my first and my only. I have to make sure he is my last. He is only now learning to love, so I have to make sure he doesn't get scared again.

As he takes a nipple in his mouth, I shiver beneath him, unable to hold in a moan.

His hands skim over my skin and make me want him more. I can't hold back the earth-shattering effect of my climax when his lips move over my clit and pleasure me.

It courses through me before he kisses me silent again. Dylan thrusts into me in one fluid motion and my body accepts him like we were meant to be.

Linking our fingers, he takes me to the peak again. Paying attention to my moans and cries of pleasure, he slows his pace, kissing me again, so I melt into him one last time before he takes me over the edge with him as he climaxes too. Sighing, the soft caress of his hands makes me snuggle deeper into him.

I never want to leave his side. Ever. And I hope I never have to.

***

THE MONTH THAT FOLLOWS THE END OF THEIR TOUR IS bliss for me. Dylan returns after the performance at the mayor's residence, and he spends most of his time with me while I prepare for my summer fashion show.

The collection is coming alive, there are a lot of dresses ready for the event already. Casey is working as a scout for models because we are looking into starting our own modeling agency alongside the brand. And I want a face for Keaton's Designs.

I go for another ultrasound because Dylan missed the first ones. We're together in the room when the doctor walks in and smiles at us. "Are you ready?" she asks.

"Yes," we chorus. Picking up a gel, the doctor motions for me to raise my shirt so she can apply some to my abdomen.

I realize I'm holding my breath when Dylan takes my hand and links our fingers, then I wait till the doctor brings the monitor to focus. I gasp when the image of a tiny human comes to focus. It's my third time watching my baby, but each time is a new miracle for me.

"He's so tiny," Dylan says, and I'm unable to hold back the excitement that courses through me. I never imagined I'd be this excited about having a kid, but being here with Dylan, watching our baby on the monitor maks me warm inside, and I instantly know I'll love it.

"Yes, it is," the doctor answers, proceeding to tell us how healthy it is and what other changes we should still expect from my body.

After the doctor's appointment, Dylan and I hang out in a cafeteria. Where silently enjoying some nice grilled chicken with roasted cauliflower.

"I'm happy, Amy."

Looking at him, I notice his relaxed appearance. His cheekbones are raised from smiling, and his voice is light. "I really am, and I was a fool not to realize sooner how much I love you."

"How did you first know it?" I ask. "How did you first know you were in love with me?"

"When I realized how miserable I was without hearing your laugh or helping you out with the tiniest of things. When it dawned on me that the reason why I was so sad was that you weren't in my life. That night when you called me, hearing your voice made my heart ache so much, and I hated that I had to hurt you, but I didn't think I was capable of feeling emotions like love."

"You're an amazing man, Dylan," I tell him, covering his hand with mine. "And I love you."

Heat radiates through me, making my grin widen.

He laughs, saying, "I'm about to do something spontaneous."

I watch him get on his feet and take off the cap on his head. "Hey everyone," he announces, instantly getting the attention of everyone in the cafeteria.

My eyes widen, and he is still smiling as he says, "I love this woman right here."

My cheeks heat up as people start to cheer, and I laugh when he starts making a sound with his lips and hands, then starts singing a famous song by musician Taylor Walker, 'Love me like you mean it'.

People are capturing the moment, and some even start singing along with him. I'm certain we'll be all over the internet by morning, but I don't mind. I'm happy, and so is Dylan. That's all that matters.

We are giggling like high school kids when we leave the cafeteria that night and head to my apartment. Dylan stays the night again, leaving early the next morning to catch his flight to Seattle where his first foundation center is opening.

Seattle is Dylan's hometown, and having his dad there with him will make a world of difference, since he wants his dad there from the start. I'm so proud of everything he's doing, and how far he's brought his passion. It feels like a long time ago when he had first shared his dreams with me, and I had done the same.

One day this week, I'm supposed to meet Mika and Lucas. They are buying a house here in New York to settle down, and I suspect they are expecting a kid soon because Mika always looks cheery and plump these days. Her glow is unmistakable.

It's evening when Casey comes to visit, and she's in a sullen mood.

"I got a divorce," she announces when I let her into my apartment. "I need a drink," she adds.

Going to my kitchen, I bring her a bottle of red wine. I can't have any, but I don't mind watching her drink while she tells me all about her experience.

"Why did he finally agree?"

She shrugs. "I guess he realized that nothing good can come from our relationship." Her expression is slack, and she adds, "I don't want to talk about it tonight, I just want to drink and hang out."

Using work stuff as a distraction, we spend the early hours of the night discussing outfit ideas for the summer collection. Casey is also quick to bring up new designs and I love that about her. She's helped the brand come alive in many ways, and we'll forever be co-owners.

After she leaves, I get on a video call with Dylan. We talk for a while till I fall asleep, listening to the sound of his voice, and the next morning, I wake up to an I love you text from him that makes me smile.

A great way to start my day, I think getting on my feet and heading for a quick shower.

25

DYLAN

Amy has no idea I'm returning to New York today and it's the first day of her summer show. My trip to Seattle to set up the foundation turned out to be a long one, and since it's Christmas Eve already, I want to surprise her.

It's been three weeks and every cell in my body is anticipating the moment when I can hug or kiss her again. There must be something on my expression because my father asks, "Excited?"

"Yes, I am," I answer, smiling. The plan to surprise Amy is an intense one. Reaching for the ring in the breast pocket of my jacket, I open the box and stare at the diamond for a while.

"It's lovely," my dad says. "I'm sure she'll love it."

"You think so?" I ask, hopeful, glancing at him briefly before looking at the ring again. "I could get something bigger ... Shinier, maybe?"

He laughs, shaking his head. "I don't think Amy cares much about the size of the ring. She cares for you, Son, not the size of the diamond or how shiny it is."

His words make sense, but I'm still a bit nervous about the entire plan.

My guys are already at the venue, I'm the last to arrive because of my flight from Seattle, but I already have it all planned out. Amy has no idea we are performing the last song at her show today. I planned it with Casey a few days ago and she put us on the list of musicians for the day.

"It'll turn out well," my father says, turning up the radio. 'Marry Me' by Jason Derulo is playing. I laugh at the encouraging sign. Taking a deep breath, I gather my wits, then count the seconds till we arrive at the venue where Casey leads us in through the back, and Amy is already on stage thanking the crowd. Catching a glimpse of her when the curtains rise, I instantly love the red figure-hugging dress she's wearing. It's long-sleeved, the red is shiny, and it shows her lovely bump.

She looks fuller than before. It's been weeks since I touched her, and my pulse just keeps racing faster.

As Amy nears the end of her speech, the lights come off on the stage, surprising her. I go on first, My jacket fully zipped up, playing the guitar with Lucas by my side, singing to the crowd that immediately starts to cheer for us.

Amy turns around, and the wide, excited look in her eyes fills me with even more courage.

Casey had planned for Chase and Jay's instruments, so they join in.

Laughing hard, Amy is framing her hands around her mouth as I walk over to her while playing the guitar. Taking the mic from her, I join Lucas in the singing. We perform the songs we had set for tonight and I love the effects Casey worked on. Glitters start to pour from above us. Amy seems to love this too because she looks up, then back at me again.

We are fully performing 'Perfect You,' the song I wrote

in Hawaii when I met her. The first one about her, even if I didn't fully know it at the time. As we reach the end of the song, there's a bridge where it's just Lucas who's singing. Taking the chance, I get on one knee, pulling out the ring box and opening it in front of her.

"I want to spend the rest of my life with you," I tell her sincerely. "I never want to be apart from you, ever again, Amy ... Say you'll marry me?"

She stares at me for the longest second of my life before nodding. Her left hand reaches for me and I slip the ring on her finger. Getting on my feet, I go in for a kiss. The crowd keeps cheering, Lucas is singing, and the moment gets more intense when I lift Amy off the ground a bit and twirl her around before setting her back on her feet.

Grinning at her, I slowly unzip my jacket and show her my T-shirt. Her laugh is priceless as she reads the words I had printed just for this occasion. Under a his and hers rings are the words "I asked and she said YES."

"What if I had said no?" she asks, as her laughter died down.

"I would have asked again..." I kiss her on the forehead, "and again..." the nose, "and again," the mouth, "as many times as it took for the answer to be the one I wanted. You are stuck with me and I'm never letting you go."

That night, we have dinner at a restaurant I had booked for the evening and it's a romantic affair, with fruit wine, roses, and dim lights.

"I can't believe this is happening," Amy tells me after we finish our meal. She had a Tasmanian salmon fillet with Dutch carrot puree, and I went for a more conventional Chinese chicken salad.

Driving around town after dinner, we end up in my suite for the night.

"We're getting married," she squeals in a tiny voice when we enter the bedroom.

Closing the door behind me, I take her in my arms for a hug. "Yes, we are," I answer. And I can't believe how happy that makes me.

"I don't want to waste any more time, Amy. I've already wasted enough. I want to be with you for the rest of our lives. You, our son, and other kids."

She laughs hard, tilting her head to one side. "Son?" she asks teasingly. "What if it's a girl?"

"It's a boy," I say with conviction.

"How can you be so sure?"

"I'm not," I say. "But I feel it." Kissing her while she's giggling, I add, "I'll love it even if it's a girl. Or twins."

Wrapping my arms around her waist, she presses another kiss to my lips before she looks into my eyes again. "I checked," she whispers. "It's a boy."

We both smile, then I turn her around so I can give her a back hug because I'm closer to her body without the baby bump in the way.

"Then I'll love him too."

Kissing the side of her neck, I close my eyes, and sigh.

I have found my happily ever after.

EPILOGUE
AMY

Dylan is performing a solo for my clothing line launch 'Bold n' Beautiful' and it's amazing hearing him sing again after the year-long break we both took from our careers. In the time I was away, Casey had managed the company while Dylan worked on promoting his foundation.

It had been a more forceful break for Dylan, because Chase had been recovering from an accident, but it had all worked out. Chase was now fully recovered and Dylan's foundation had grown.

Now HeartsWithYou has counseling centers in almost fifteen states across the country and an online presence for people who need them in other parts of the world. Dylan's influence, alongside the band's joint efforts, makes it possible for the foundation to garner many donations and support, and I am certain in five years, it will be bigger than it is right now.

I'm waving my hands in the air and singing along to Dylan's lyrics. He has our son on his right lap while he plays the guitar, and at some point, he stops so Collin can play some strings on the guitar too.

My almost two-year-old is a genius when it comes to guitars. I guess he gets it from his dad. At random times, I would catch Collin staring at Dylan's guitar, and sometimes, he plays the strings even though his tone makes no sense yet.

With time, he'll find his own passion. Even if it's not music, I will support whatever it is.

After the show ends, as the crowd is cheering, I'm doing the same because I'm in love with both men on the stage right now, and I know they both love me back. Getting on the stage to join them, and I take the mic to give the thank you speech again.

Keaton Designs is now one of the most successful designer brands in the States. I already have celebrities lined up to work with for the upcoming Grammy and Emmy awards.

Last week, I secured a deal with a movie producer to design costumes for his set, and I can't wait to launch into that project too. It is going to be a busy year for me, and I am looking forward to it.

After the show, we drive to our private beach house at Port Jefferson, New York. Lucas and Mika are there, alongside July, their one-year-old. Jay and Chase are joining us too. July plays with Collin the entire night while the rest of us enjoy our time together.

It's a cool night, and the coziness of the estate where the house is located gives us a serenity away from the usual buzz of New York City. Dylan purchased the house after our wedding, almost two years ago, and since then it has been our haven away from the hassles of work.

Leaving the living room for a bit, I check on Collin and

July in the children's room and find them both asleep on the bed, their hands wrapped around each other's bodies.

A smile forms on my lips as I move closer to the bed to pull the sheets over their bodies. Dylan comes into the room, putting a hand on my back.

Sighing, I lean into his light caress after making sure both kids are in a comfortable sleeping position.

"They look cozy," he whispers, and I nod.

"They do."

Leaving the room, we end up on our balcony. I can still hear laughter from downstairs where the others are having fun, but I want this time alone with Dylan, so I lean closer to him for a hug and let his warmth seep through my body.

"I have to travel in a few weeks," he tells me. "To Africa this time."

"We're expanding the foundation?" I ask.

"It's a charity concert, the band is performing. Ken thinks it's a great idea."

"I think so, too."

I wish I could go with him on this trip but there is a lot of work to be done with Keaton's too.

"Hopefully, I can come with you on your next trip," I say.

"Yeah ... I'd love to have you with me," he agrees, kissing my temple.

After a second of silence, as I start humming a song from Soul Sounds' latest album, Dylan joins me, singing it for some time before lifting me off my feet and twirling me around till I giggle hard and struggle to break free from him.

Laughing, we enter the bedroom and close the balcony door.

In the next minute, I'm in his arms, and his lips are on

mine, kissing me senseless. Putting my hands around his neck, I lift myself on tiptoe and give into the kiss.

As he tilts his head to one side, I slip my tongue into his mouth and he meets my thrust with his own tongue, deepening the kiss.

My hands move down his back, pressing him closer to me while I back him toward the bed. Smiling, I let my hands trail down his chest, and he groans in response to it.

"You're tempting me," he whispers when our lips part so we can both gasp for air.

"I know," I say in a sexy voice, moving back from him so I can push him to the bed gently, straddling him.

Lowering myself onto his body, I slide a hand down his chest again so I can slip it under his T-shirt.

"I love how you respond," I say, then give him a sexy grin before bringing my lips to his for another kiss. Our passion still burns as bright as it did the very first day I was in his arms, and everything else was perfect.

"And I love you," he answers.

I've found the love of my life. My first, my only, my all. And there's no going back now.

www.ingramcontent.com/pod-product-compliance
Lightning Source LLC
Chambersburg PA
CBHW021356150726
47989CB00005B/2264